Double

Either I was in need of a haircut or the nights were drawing in. Sitting in my anything but large office I looked out of the window that urgently needed cleaning to the Bass Rock, which also was in urgent need of a wash. Rain was not so far away. To add to my misery I turned to my office bills for October 1997. Perhaps a cup of coffee would cheer me up. I rose at the same time that there was a knock on the door, and before I had time to invite in my unexpected visitor, the door was pushed slightly open.

"Skivving as usual" the head said that peered at me from around the corner of the open door.

Instantly I recognised the face and the voice, "Mark Lauder! Where the hell have you been hiding?" I swept my hand in a welcoming gesture, "Come in. What brings you to see your old buddy?" Suddenly my day was bright.

Mark gave a sheepish grin and sat himself down. He like myself was in his mid thirties, but much heavier built, possibly through eating less rubbish.

"I think it might be what I can do for you." He stared around the office, "Not doing too well, I would say."

"Oh I get by." I did not want to get into telling him that I was now quite well off as a result of my saving the two sons of the tycoon Mr Desmond, which reminded me that I must pay them a visit in the USA, especially Sarah their chaperone.

I sat back smiling, "So what is it you can do for me?"

Mark pulled at his ear, clearly embarrassed by what he was about to say. "Since I left," he hesitated smiling awkwardly, "since I was thrown off the Force..."

"That was a mistake and we all know it, except Thomson

that is." I assured him.

Mark nodded. "Well to cut a long story short I do part time work as an independent security guard, and this job has come up that needs two, so I thought of you."

"I'm flattered. Or is it because you think I need the money and will work for next to nothing?"

"How did you know my name was Nothing?" Mark grinned, "Seriously though, the job is only for two weeks. Do you know Muir of the building consortium?"

I nodded, "Doesn't everyone?"

"Right. Well David Campbell, old Muir's managing director contacted me. Seems the old boy is none too well and needs someone to keep an eye on him while Campbell pulls off another big deal for him. He is already in the Borders working on a project."

Mark saw me wrinkle my brows, "I'm not the nursemaid kind, Mark."

He shook his head, "Nothing like that..well almost nothing like that."

When I remained silently sceptical, he continued. "I don't know all the ins and outs of high finance etc. except Campbell has told me that my…our duty is to keep nosey reporters away until the deal is clinched. Seems the Press have got hold of a story that the Boss Man is in a bad way, and Campbell might not be competent to deal with the situation. Campbell's story is that his boss only needs a rest. Old Muir is holed up in his own house out by the Lammermuirs. Strangely, Campbell insisted that on no account should Mr Muir's grandchildren be allowed to see him. Seemingly, he dotes on them, but I believe they don't give two brass farthings for the old boy, only his money. Okay?"

It sounded strange but I nodded my understanding.

Mark glanced at his watch." Campbell is to meet us at the house at three o'clock. That will give you four hours to get ready."

"Ready for what?"

"Oh it's a live in job. We are there 24/7. Between us that is."

I sat back in my chair studying the man across the desk. "And should I say no, what then?"

"I'd be in deep shit for I have already agreed to do the job. I was sure you needed the work pal, so I gave Campbell your name."

"And I could give you one as well."

Mark's eyes opened wide. "You're not going to turn me down?" I saw the look of disappointment on his face. "I really need the work, West. It's not been easy," he splayed his hands. "Well after you know what. And there's wee Kirsty to think about."

"You really know how to punch below the belt," I laughed. "How is the wee girl now?"I asked, referring to his daughter.

"Fine. She'll be seven next month."
I whistled. "Seven already. How time flies."

Mark nodded and looked at his watch, "Which reminds me, time is getting short. So what do you say? Will you take the job? The money's good, for you that is, since you'll be doing the most hours."

He waited for my reaction. "Meaning?"

Mark chuckled. "Can you do five at night 'till eight in the morning? My sister Margaret looks after Kirsty when she comes out of school until I get home about five ..ish. I know you will be doing the most hours but you'll have your own room, and I don't expect you'll have your sleep disturbed too often. Any reporters, if any, are likely to call during the day. So it will be up to me to satisfy their curiosity."

It didn't seem to be too stressful, and it took little imagination to realise the man needed the work. "Okay. You've got yourself a deal."

The relief spreading over my friends face convinced me that I had done the decent thing, more so for his young daughter, now without the benefit of a mother these past years.

Mark rose and drew out a slip of paper from his pocket. "That's the address, though I expect you'll have an idea where this particular tycoon lives," he chuckled, turning at the door to add "see you there, and thanks again pal."

The Lammermuir Hills looked sullenly down at me as I approached Muir House this wet and dismal afternoon, and although not quite knowing why, I shuddered at the omen.

Perhaps I should not have taken the job, but the thought of how hard a time Mark had had after what to me had been an unfair dismissal, and his having to bring up a wee girl without a mother, made me think again.

A solitary car stood in the long gravel driveway, and I pulled up beside it and made a dash for the front door before the rain soaked me through.

Mark answered my call on the doorbell his face lighting up at seeing me, he took a step back to let me in against the driving rain. "I was hoping you wouldn't change your mind."

"Wee Kirsty did that for you," I answered, my eyes on the large reception hall and the winding staircase leading from it.

"Mr Campbell phoned me just before I left." Mark led me to a door leading into a kitchen boasting all the most up to date gadgets imaginable, and some I hadn't known had been invented. "Coffee?" he headed for a pot on the stove, "Seemingly Mr Campbell has been called away urgently to the Borders and has left me to do the honour of introducing you to our client." Smiling he handed me a coffee, "Sugar's over there." He pointed to a worktop with even more up to date gadgets.

I helped myself to sugar. "Seems you already know your way around."

"Only just. I got here about an hour ago. I've been up to see the old boy. I didn't want him to think he had burglars."

"Wouldn't surprise me if he did, seeing as there seems to be no CCTV cameras outside, or in here as a matter of fact," I looked around me, "You would think that a man as wealthy as the man upstairs would have this place covered in no small way."

"Perhaps he doesn't think them necessary," Mark chuckled. "I mean him being as wealthy as he is reputed to be, he might just replace whatever might be stolen."

Mark put down his empty coffee cup. "If you're finished I'll take you up to meet our esteemed employer."

The bedroom was large, a consol TV stood in a corner; built- in wardrobes on three walls, a settee and bedside chair. A large window gave an interrupted view of the Lammermuirs' A set of drawers by the bed, in which sat a man that I judged to be around sixty years old, but by his physique, too healthy to be bedridden, but then again looks can be deceptive.

Andrew Muir looked up from where he had been reading a book, his stare sweeping over Mark to rest upon myself, though it was Mark he addressed. "So this is the other one. It takes two to look after an old man, Eh?"

I felt rather than saw Mark stiffen.

"We are to take shifts to make sure you don't sleep walk sir." I ventured with a smile to ease Mark's uneasiness.

Andrew Muir did not respond to my humour, instead he swung his stare to the man beside me. "When do I get fed? Am I to starve in my own house?"

This was a man I realised who was accustomed to being the boss and having his own way.

"Livvy will be along shortly to make you a meal sir."

The man in the bed grunted. "Make sure it's pork chops, and not the rubbish she served for lunch." He lifted his book, a sure sign the interview was over.

We had reached the kitchen before Mark asked. "Well, what do you think of our Mr Muir?"

I shrugged. "Didn't ask who or what I was." I helped myself to a coffee from the simmering pot.

"Didn't need to, I told him all about you."

"And I still got the job?" I chuckled.

"We better not louse it up West. I really need the money."

So this was why my pal had been so nervous upstairs. He really must be finding it hard to make ends meet. It could not be easy having a reputation as a bent cop, something that I myself did not believe.

I took a sip of coffee. "No worries pal we'll get through it alright."

He smiled a slight assurance at me, glancing at his watch. "Livvy should be here any time now."

"Seems you're right for once." I cocked my ear, "sound like a car."

The woman who entered the kitchen was in her mid thirties, something similar to that of Mark and myself.

"This is West, Livvy, my partner in crime." Mark introduced me with a smile.

"Pleased to meet you Livvy." I too smiled and stepped forward to take one of the two plastic shopping bags she was carrying.

"Thanks, West." She put her bag down on the work top near the fridge. She turned to look at me and I hoped she liked what she saw, for to say she was pretty would have been an understatement, if not downright insulting. Wavy brown hair with deep blue sparkling eyes.

She cocked her head. "Have you been up to see our lordship? I know that I'm expected to cook for him, but treating me like a servant as well, the stuck up old bugger, that's going a bit over the score."

I laughed, and watched her put away the groceries from the shopping bags. "I hope you got him pork chops?"

"Yes, he's expecting them Livvy," Mark added.

Livvy swung round. "Well he will be disappointed, for he's getting chicken pieces and like it."

It was the way she said it that left me with no doubt that this was a lady to be reckoned with.

"I hope you like chicken, West?" she addressed me, her tone warm.

I nodded. "My best food. Suits my personality."

"Don't let him fool you, Livvy, he was a pretty good detective in the Force." Mark said in my defence.

"So you were both upholders of the law." Livvy nodded her understanding. And when neither of us chose to further enlighten her, she turned back to the worktop. "Seems it's only cops that are allowed to ask 'a few questions'", she sighed.

"Well, I best be on my way. I will leave you two to face his nibs up there when he sees there's no pork chops, just chicken."

"Two if you count me," I said.

"What did the boss man say when he saw that it wasn't pork chops?" I asked when Livvy returned with the tray.

She sat the tray down. "I asked for pork chops, he threw at me. So I told him chicken or starve."

Amused I waited until she turned round. "You'll get your marching orders. That guy upstairs is used to getting what he wants."

"He almost got something he didn't want." Livvy threw a glance at her watch, and stepped towards the door. "Yours is in the micro. All you have to do is heat it. OK"

She halted in the doorway. "Sorry, I didn't mean to take it out on you."

"Understood."

"See you tomorrow then." Her smile lit up her face.

For a moment I stood there drinking in this lovely creature standing there, and mumbled a, "yes I suppose so."

"Good." Then she was gone.

I thought it best to find out how the old pain in the posterior was fairing before sitting down to my own meal. I knocked and entered before he had time to call out.

"Your meal all right sir?" I asked, preparing for a tirade about the absence of pork chops. To my surprise he nodded and wiped his lips with a napkin.

"Very satisfactory, Barns. Hope the chops tomorrow are as tasty as this chicken." He drew me a look and instantly I knew this man in the bed was playing a game.

Was he as ill as I was led to believe? Or was there more to it?"

Chapter 2

I yawned into my watch at having slightly overslept, rose and started my ablutions. Mark arrived first, and by the time I had finished, I heard Livvy's car draw up.

A hint of trepidation in his voice Mark asked, "Everything go all right, West?"

Obviously this job meant a great deal to the man, and any hint that anything, however slight might go wrong had him worried.

Livvy said her good mornings to us both and we followed her into the kitchen.

"Too lazy to put the kettle on, West Barns? Or is that not in your remit?"

I made a face at Mark who gestured his surprise. "Got out of the wrong side of bed this morning did you?" I asked attempting to sound cheerful. "It can be painful if the bed's against the wall."

"Bog off West I'm in no mood for your stupid wit."

"What's wrong Livvy? West's only trying to be nice."

"That type of nice I can do without at this time of the morning, especially after a puncture."
"So that's it. Did you change the spare by yourself?"

Livvy swung round on Mark, "and you can bug off as well Mark Lauder."

We both thought it time to leave the kitchen to cat woman.

"Don't fancy Mr Muir chances if he rubs her the wrong way this morning," Mark frowned.

Breakfast over, and Livvy long gone, I turned to Mark as I was about to leave. "I don't have much on today that I know of Mark, so I'll come back a bit early and let you go if you like."

"Thanks pal I know Margaret will appreciate it, and I can take Kirsty out somewhere for a wee while."

"Good. See around three ish."

I should not have made that promise, long before I reached the gravel path leading to the house upon my return about three o'clock, I spied a full horde of journalist clustered around the front door with a much exasperated Mark Lauder vainly trying to hold them and their questions at bay.

I reached the rearmost and roughly pushed the first of the reporters out of the way, holding up my Private Investigator card in an imitation of a police one and shouted at them to make way. Finally I made the open front door.

"Am I glad to see you," Mark shouted at me, and together we managed to close the door.

"Serves me right." Mark gulped the words at me. "Never should have opened the damned thing. I thought if I gave them the story Mr Campbell told me to tell them, that they might be satisfied and bog off. How wrong was I."

We made our way to the kitchen where Livvy was already preparing the afternoon snack before starting to prepare the evening one.

"How come you got past that lot out there?" I jerked a thumb in the direction of the front door.

She turned and held up a key. "Back door. Very appropriate for serving wenches don't you think?" Completely unfazed by what was going on outside.

"Got a spare one?" I asked hopefully.

"You don't need one, usually by the time you get here the press have gone."

"That's me told." I made a face.

Mark laughed. "Maybe you can let me out that way, Livvy?" He picked up his coat.

"Jeez, that's some coat Mark, it must have cost a fortune and you said you were skint."

"It's called Canada Goose from an admirer," he chuckled.

"Is that what I'm having a gander at!" I laughed.

"Very punny," Mark said dead pan. "As you say I could never afford anything like this."

"Some admirer," I said enviously. This time we all laughed.

It was close on three in the afternoon next day, and strangely there were not so many reporters about when I first heard the sound of a motor bike. Once again having no urgent business to attend to in my office or out of it for that matter, I came early to the house in order to let Mark spend a bit more time at home with his daughter.

My first instinct was to take a look out of one of the front windows before answering the door.

"Who is it?" Livvy called out from the kitchen.

"A boy on a motor bike," I called back, making for the door.

Almost immediately the unfortunate boy was pounced upon by the few remaining vultures. I swung the door open and before the youngster knew what was happening had hauled him inside by the collar of his black leather jacket.

"Jesus! What's going on?" The startled boy stared up at me.

"Don't worry kid, they do that to all of us, it's our sandwiches from Martins they're after." This only served to further puzzle him as he swung his backpack off his shoulders in company with a bewildered expression. "I only came to deliver these to Mr Muir and take back the previous ones," he said delving into the bag, and extracting a buff coloured folder.

"I don't have any sandwiches," he added with an apologetic look.

"What! No sandwiches!" It was Livvy entering from the kitchen who spoke. "What are we to do, West? Starve? And that old man upstairs lying waiting for you," she drew closer to the boy, before letting out a laugh at the youngsters look of dubiety.

"We're only winding you up, kid," I apologised, thinking we had gone too far.

"Have you time for a cuppa?" Livvy asked still finding the situation amusing.

"Maybe…just.."

"Of course you do. Follow me."

Jamie had still not stopped shaking by the time he was on his second chocolate biscuit. Not from our unusual greeting, or the reporters outside, but from the way Livvy was treating him, having the poor lad wondering what she would do next. I could almost see those brain cells reaching boiling point, that's should brain cells have a boiling point and that his hair would stand straight up at any second.

"Another cup Jamie?"

Jamie choked a "yes"

I thought it time to rescue this innocent young man, though no doubt he would hate me for it. Who could blame him? Besides, I felt a twinge of jealousy that it wasn't me that was the precipitant of such attention. "If you find the strength to give me that folder for Mr Muir I'll take it to him while you enjoy another cuppa."

For a moment Jamie looked dazed, then came back from Livvy's world to hand me the folder. "Mr Muir takes this one and I have to get the one Mr Campbell left for him to sign earlier in the week, and take that one back to Mr Blair the accountant at the office."

"How about a piece of my cherry cake?" Livvy asked the bewildered boy whose trembling hands handed me the brown folder.

"A piece of your cherry.." Jamie choked.

"Cake." I completed the sentence for him.

Speechless, Jamie could only manage a nod.

The boss was watching TV when I entered folder in hand. "I believe your office would like you to peruse these, sir," I said politely.

"Mm? What?" Muir tore his eyes away from the screen, and I handed him the folder.

For a moment or two he just sat there in bed staring at it, then finally having made up his mind pointed to a desk in the corner of the room. "There's a folder over there that has to be returned to the office," he threw at me sharply.

I crossed to the desk and lifted the folder, and on my way back to the bedside asked. "Is there anything I can get you sir while I am here?"

Muir looked annoyed. "Give it here." He snapped his fingers and all but tore the folder from my grasp.

"No. Just give this to whoever has called."

It was the way he had of saying 'no' that made me glad that I wasn't a full time employee.

Ten minutes later a bewildered young biker gunned his way up the driveway.

Livvy turned from where she had watched her dotting admirer depart. "Do you think I was a bit hard on the laddie?" she asked, with an amused grin.

"A bit. The wee soul didn't know if he was Arthur or Martha at times the way you teased him. Do you always do that to innocent young men," I asked seriously. Thinking of how many hearts she might have broken.

She laughed. "Not only innocent ones, West barns." She changed quickly. "Now I too must leave you. Dinner is already prepared for you both."

"Cheers," I said while she made herself ready to leave.

That night I switched on the TV. "Oh no not another fantasy film," I moaned. "it makes a change from cookery programmes I suppose." I had run out of snarky comments, when it happened that around nine o'clock I head the front doorbell ring. Thinking that it was the odd reporter, some of who really were, I cautiously took a peek through the spy hole only to have my worst fears realised. Again the bell rang, impatiently this time, followed by an equally impatience voice howling to open the door and quick. Knowing I had little choice I swung the door open but only just to find a shoe wedged in the space.

"Who are you? And why are you not letting us in? We are Mr Muir's grandchildren after all."

The voice may be small but the owner sure as hell wasn't. No doubt in today's parlance to say this female creature who stood before me, and a little more besides, was obese, stout, fat or even diet challenged may be wrong, but whatever may be politically correct, the result was the same. I knew I must not leap to the assumption that the girl's figure was the result of over indulgence should her condition be a result of her genes or hormones or whatever else that was amiss, however this miss was about to throw her weight around and me too, should she not gain admittance.

"We are Mr Muir's grandchildren." The squeaky voice had me turn my attention to the weedy boy who stood beside Miss Cairngorms. "We heard he was ill, so we came as quickly as possible."

I tried to push the door a little but to no avail. "I'm sorry but the doctor says that Mr Muir has not to have any visitors," I lied.

"Can we not see Gramps for just a little while?" Weedy asked, in that same squeaky voice.

"I'm sorry I'm afraid not."

"You will be if you don't open this door!" Mountain woman pushed at the door and it took all my manly strength to hold her to a draw.

"Never mind Hazel, we'll phone Gramps and he's sure to let us see him." Squeaky said.

Hazel? I thought how appropriate a name for this particular nut.

Reluctantly Hazel took a step back. "Okay we'll be back mister, and when Gramps finds out how you treated us, you'll be looking for another job." Another step back and she asked, "What's you name by the way?"

I shook my head. "No, it's not by the way. Not even Mr By the Way to you. So I bid you both a good evening." I shut the door with a thud.

Next morning Mark's eyes opened wide in consternation when I told him about our unwelcome visitors.

"You didn't let them in?" His voice was almost a shout.

"No, the orders were that no one was to disturb our esteemed leader." My answer seemed to calm him.

"What about him upstairs?" Livvy stuck her thumb up at the ceiling." Did he hear them?"

I shook my head. "If he did, he didn't call out."

"I still think there's more to our Mr Muir." Livvy looked at both of us in turn. "He's anything but bedridden."

I nodded. "You're not wrong Livvy",I swung to Mark. "Is there something you're not telling us, pal?"

Mark made a face. "No. All Campbell told me was to keep reporters and his grandkids away."

We left it at that.

The following day, as I had a contract with the local council to find out who were responsible for unlawful fly tipping, and having already made Mark aware of this, I set out to do my good neighbour bit.

There was not much doing business wise in the office, so after a cup of coffee I set out in the afternoon to find the culprits, a couple of local cowboys.

Just outside of Haddington I drew up a little way from the yard they used and camera at the ready waited for them to depart.

After an hour of impatient waiting there was still no sign of their truck leaving with its usual load of rubbish to dispose of. Had I got it wrong? It was this day last week that they had left on their unlawful errand. It was now a few minutes short of four o'clock and if they did not soon leave I'd be late back to let Mark finish his shift at the house.

Ten minutes later they did leave, and I started a cautious tail after them. Fifteen minutes later I was still following the loaded truck deep into the countryside; a different road from last week.

It was quite difficult to follow on this quiet country road without being seen. Not knowing the roads too well I was never sure what was round the next bend so slowed down even more. It was just as well that I did so, for rounding the next bend I glimpsed the tail end of the truck disappear down a rutted lane. Now I had to stop, for there was no way I could follow without raising suspicion. How far, and where the road led I had no idea. Then to my relief the truck halted and so did I.

When the truck began to tip its load I got out of the car, and hidden by a few bushes, I got my first photo. Another few and I was out of there. Too late I was seen, and the first big bruiser came after me. I ran, but not quite as fast as the bruiser, and he had me by the arm before I got any further. Fortunately his pal was still unaware of what was happening, so I had only this gorilla to deal with. Only I thought. He must be about six feet twelve! So I took the only option left to me, I hit him with my camera, and didn't wait to see what would develop and I didn't mean photo wise. He gave a yelp at my blow, giving me just enough time to break free and run or should I say hobble on my gammy leg, the result of an old police injury, to my car.

The blow however was not enough to slow him down, and I saw the look of anger when he caught up with me, and in the near distance his pal coming to his aid.

I swung my weapon again. This time he ducked but I managed to land a blow again that once more gave me time to reach my car.

I swore in anticipation of the engine failing to start, but much to my relief it did first time and putting it into reverse was out of there before I could say I required the toilet or words to that affect.

A few nervous miles later I pulled up. It was already a few minutes short of five o'clock, I would be late to take over from Mark.

I pressed the buttons on my mobile and waited.
Eventually I heard Mark's voice on the other end. "Mark,
it's me," I quickly informed him, swiftly glancing into my
rear mirror for any sign of the Men in Black. "Sorry, I'll be
a bit late in getting back. Can you wait?"

"How long is a bit late?"

"Fifteen minutes. Maybe less."

"OK, pal."

The phone went dead and I got out of there before I did.

It took all the strength of my windscreen wipers to let me
see where I was going. The monsoon season had finally
reached the Lammermuirs this dismal October evening.

I brought the car to a halt in the empty driveway,
evidently Mark had not hung around to await my arrival,
nor could I blame him. At best he would only have left by
a few minutes, though I had not passed him on the way.

Lights shone in each room lending a homely glow amid
the mini storm.

Closing the front door behind me, I first made for the
kitchen, throwing off my wet jacket before turning on the
micro oven and setting it with the evening meal for his
nibs upstairs.

By the time I had taken my own meal already prepared
by Livvy from the fridge, the micro had done its job. I took
the meal out and replaced it with my own.

Holding the tray in one hand I knocked on the boss's
door, entering with "Your evening meal Mr Muir. How are
you today?" Halting in surprise at the sight of the empty
bed, and thinking he may be in the toilet I set down the
tray by the bedside.

A couple of minutes later, convinced that the old man
was not in the toilet or if he was, had fallen asleep on the

job so to speak, or at worst had passed away on his throne, I gave the door a timid knock, with an "Are you all right Mr Muir, sir?"

When there was still no answer I gently pushed the door open, expecting to hear an outburst of indignation from within, instead there was no reply. The toilet was empty.

Now convinced there was something wrong I took a quick look around. Opening the wardrobe I found that Mr Muir's clothes were still there, as were his undergarments etc. in the chest of drawers.

Returning to the bed I pulled back the pillows and dishevelled bedclothes but found nothing. A book he had been reading lay on the floor, beside it a broken pair of spectacles and just sticking out from beneath the bed an empty syringe. I stood back and let out a low whistle, obviously our Mr Muir was a diabetic, which meant that he had not left voluntarily. Nor was it likely that Mark would have taken him for a sightseeing tour in his PJs.

A further search of the room revealed nothing of any significance.

That Mark had not contacted me was proof enough that he was in some sort of trouble.

Also I was suspicious of the Boss man himself, for I was not completely convinced that he was indeed bedridden. But where did it leave me? If Muir was abducted, and as I had not passed any car on the way here it had to have been close to the time I phoned saying that I would be a bit late on arriving. This had me thinking, had I been on time, it could easily have been me that was missing instead of Mark, and had that been the case, I at least would have a better idea of what was going on.

Now I had to work out what had really happened. If Mark had heard a car approach he might have mistaken it for mine, perhaps opened the door for me in his haste to be away home to Kirsty. Taken by surprise he could easily have been overpowered, but not by one man alone. Even so it would have taken two, one to have taken care of Mr Muir.

On impulse I headed for the kitchen smelling the dinner for which I was no longer hungry.

I shook my head. The back door key was still on its hook. But didn't Livvy say she had one? Or was this it?

I gave it a quarter of an hour before I phoned Mark for a second time, but again there was no reply. Now more worried I phoned his home, working out what I would tell Margaret should Mark not be there.

Margaret's voice greeted me from the other end. "Oh it's you West, Kirsty and I are wondering where her daddy is. He's never been this late before."

The woman sounded worried and I did not blame her, but what to say so as not to further worry her I did not know. Eventually I said, finding it none too easy to lie to this kind lady, "Mark's been held up here, Margaret. He's asked me to phone you and say he will be a bit late and can you look after Kirsty for tonight as he expects by the time he gets through with Mr Muir it will be past Kirsty's bedtime." I swallowed and hoped this lady would do the same with my lies.

"Ok West. I'll take Kirsty to school in the morning. Tell Mark not to worry."

I gave a deep sigh of relief. At least this would give me a little breathing space before I had to phone her again, and this time with the truth if Mark was still not to the fore.

Now it was time to phone the police, as the quicker they were aware of Muir and Mark's disappearance the better chance they had of finding them.

Next, believing there was no need to run up a bill by using my own mobile I phoned David Campbell from the house phone. The voice that answered my greeting was sharp and precise.

"West Barns? You're the one who is helping Mark Lauder to look after my boss, I believe."

"Yes, Mr Campbell, I am." At the silence on the other end, I continued, "I'm afraid I have some bad news Mr Campbell, both Mark and Mr Muir are missing." I got no further.

"Missing! What the hell do you mean by missing?"

Although I had never met this man his manner had me instantly disliking him. "Well, I sure as hell don't mean I've misplaced them," I bit back. I went on to explain what had happened.

When I had finished the voice was no longer harsh, authoritative, but instead spoke as if still digesting what I had told him and mulling over its implications. "You think my boss has been kidnapped?"

A little angry at his lack of concern at Mark's disappearance, I replied. "It's a possibility. Thanks to the Press quite a number of people knew he was here."

"Okay" Campbell said quietly. "I suppose you have contacted the police?"

I answered yes.

The voice returned to its normal severity. "Give them my number. I don't want to come back up from here if at all possible. The Boss will not be too happy if I have to come up there. And you keep me informed at what's going on."

I would dearly loved to have searched the house for some clue as to the boss's disappearance but I didn't want to be caught in the act or accused by the police of being somehow involved in old Muir's disappearance. It was just as well, for sooner than I had expected I heard the sound of cars approaching, and I hoped it would not be the obnoxious DI Robert Thomson who would be in charge. I was wrong. Thomson all but pushed me aside, surveying the spacious hall around him and me at the same time when he made his grand entrance.

"Not West Barns? Well! Well! Well! Why have I the pleasure of finding you here Barns?"

"The pleasures all mine, Inspector,"I retorted.

Thomson took a few quick steps further into the hallway taking in the winding staircase and rooms above, to the lounge and kitchen. "I'm told Muir the construction mogul has gone missing. Very careless of you West. Of course you never could do anything right when on the Force without your brother's help. Could you?"

Thomson took a few steps closer to the lounge door and took a peek inside. He turned.

"Sinclair take your men and search the place top to bottom. Miss nothing."

When the man whom he had addressed as Sinclair started off to do his lordships bidding, I said as calmly as I could. "There's no one here Thomson. I've already looked."

Thomson drew me a look of disdain. "Let the Pros do their job West. Now tell me exactly what has happened."

When I had finished, Thomson fixed his eyes on the ceiling in a gesture of disbelief.

"You're telling me you're not in charge, it's Mark Lauder? Well! Well!" he turned to stare at me. "One former bent cop and one with a bent leg!" His laughter had those around stop what they were doing.

I chose to ignore his so called witticism, while he continued. "I won't be surprised if you two are not in this together."

I could see that my failure to rise to his bait annoyed him. He spun on his heel barking out orders to his minions, quickly turning back to fix a hostile eye on me. "You have ten minutes to put your things together and get out of here Barns. This is now a suspected crime scene, therefore if you don't want to spend the remainder of the night behind bars, make yourself scarce. Don't worry we know where to find you." And abruptly turned back to hurl further instructions to what looked like a far from happy crew.

Next morning I left early to let Livvy know what had happened and to warn her about Thomson, though I believed this girl could give as much as she got. When Thomson had asked about Livvy I had truthfully told him I did not know anything beyond her making the meals for Mr Muir and myself.

After waiting ten minutes in the lay by on the deserted country road I spotted Livvy's little red Mini. I got out and waved her down. At first I thought she was not about to slacken her speed until recognising me, she quickly brought her car to a halt.

Livvy wound down her window and stared up at me, a puzzled expression on her face.

"Morning, Livvy," I cheerily greeted her.

"What the hell are you doing away out here, West Barns?"

I drew closer. "There's been some sort of an incident up at the house after you left last night. Mark and Mr Muir are missing."

"Missing!"

She sounded alarmed and I went on to inform her of what I knew.

"Mark. He's missing too?"

"Afraid so. I don't know what the hell's going on."

"Does Kirsty and her aunt know about this?"

I shook my head. "I fobbed Margaret off last night with a story about Mark working late."

I glanced at my watch, "Although I think the cops will have told her by this time."

Livvy stared at the windscreen. "I hope he's all right and nothing has happened to him, for the wee girl has suffered enough with the loss of one parent."

She turned her head to look up at me. "If it's abduction what do you think will happen to Mark? I mean..he's not involved. Is he?"

"No. Mark would not get mixed up in anything like that. I know him too well. He may have had a raw deal and a hard time since leaving the Force but he'd not risk doing anything illegal, or the chance of losing Kirsty. That wee lassie means the world to him."

My answer seemed to calm Livvy down. "I'm glad you said that West."

Can I ask a favour?" I asked apprehensively.

Livvy drew me a look. "Depends."

"If you have the back door key, would you lend it to me?"

Her hesitation had me thinking that she thought I was somewhat involved. "If it will help." She rummaged through her handbag and handed me the key.

"It will. I hope," I said, but only half hopefully. "I'll let you know how I get on."

She switched the engine back on. "Same here with this delectable Detective Thomson, you have warned me about." Then she was gone up the muddy track to meet with Mr Sherlock Holmes junior.

Chapter3

My destination now, was to Muir Constructions, Edinburgh, and I hoped that I might just get there before the police. Perhaps I would if Thomson had elected personally to interview Livvy at the old man's home.

On the way there, I mulled over what had happened, and one of the things that worried me was why should someone want to abduct so prominent a person? He was wealthy of course, but how could they go about it? Usually abduction was between the abducted person's family and themselves, with warnings not to alert the police, except here everyone from the police to the Press were aware of it.

If and when a ransom was asked for, how was it to be paid? I just couldn't see Miss Cairngorms or her weedy brother handling this side of things, but stranger things had happened when money was involved.

That Mark was not involved went without saying. Where was he? And was he all right?

No doubt Thomson would have already started interviewing Livvy by this time, and if I was not mistaken had included her as a suspect. I imagined that lady's reaction to this if he had.

At Muir and Co. I was shown into the office of Henry Blair chief accountant, a balding middle aged man, who greeted me with a look that said 'please, not more questions'.

Reluctantly he invited to me to have a seat in an office I should have expected to have been much larger for a man in his position. Introductions over, I got straight to the point.

"Doubtless you are aware of Mr Muir's disappearance, Mr Blair."

The man nodded and gave a sign of impatience. "I have already told the police this morning all I know. They have scarcely left."

"I know," I apologised. "But I was employed to look after Mr Muir and seemingly I have failed."

"You blame yourself for what has happened?" he looked at me not quite understanding why I should think to hold myself responsible.

"My partner is also missing, Mr Blair, therefore the onus is on me to find them both."

The chief accountant tapped his desk with a pencil. "I see. What do you want to know?"

Doubtless the police would have already asked him these same questions that I was about to ask, however I had to know and a little besides, if it in any way was going to help.

"Who benefits should anything have happened to the old man?"

"You mean his demise? That is what you mean Mr West?" he stared at me slyly.

"Ok. If they don't find the old codger alive, who inherits?"

My apparent insensitivity appeared to anger him and I thought I had blown my chances of getting anything at all out of him.

Dropping his pencil he drew a sheet of paper towards him, and pretended to study it, until saying without looking up. "His grandchildren of course…Hazel and…"

"I know, we've already met."

Blair set down the sheet of paper. "Then you will know they could not do anything so vile to their grandfather.

They dote on him as he does them."

"No. And I can't see them involving anyone else." I changed tact. "Do you think this present construction deal has anything to do with it? It seems to mean a lot to some people, especially to Mr Muir, at least enough to feign illness."

"What do you mean feign an illness? Mr Muir wa…is ill. He only required a few days rest. Mr Campbell is looking after the business for him until his return."

"Let's say something did happen to your boss. Who runs the whole caboodle?"

Blair looked stunned by the question never until this moment of having given it a thought.

"David Campbell, naturally. After all he is managing director."

"And with this added responsibility comes an increase in salary no doubt?"

Angry now, Blair stood up. "I think you have gone quite far enough Mr West," he choked. "I'm sure you can find your own way out."

Perhaps now was the time to use that back door key that Livvy had given me. However it was not to be as the next day the powers that be of the local council wished to see for themselves the evidence I had gathered against the illegal fly-tippers, so it was late evening before I reached home after attending to a few more important matters such as groceries and the toilet. Too late that night to go house hunting.

Although thoroughly tired I managed to scrape up a meal, scrape being the operative word, most of the meal having stuck to the bottom of the pan. Finished, and with only a couple of indigestion tablets to swallow for dessert I flopped down on the settee, remote controlled the TV, and flipped through a few hundred cookery and so called reality shows, the reality being there were not reality at all, just stupid twenty and thirty somethings in it for the money. "Get a real job!" I hurled at the screen, then sat back laughing at my own absurdity.

Tomorrow night I told myself, tomorrow night I'd try and find out what I could if anything in the big house of the big man himself, which I should have taken the time to do before contacting the police, but I had wanted the Law to know as soon as possible of the suspected kidnap and assure them it was not just a missing persons case. I also hoped to find something out before Thomson did.

Around six o'clock the next evening I called on Margaret and Kirsty.

"I thought I'd call to see how you both were."

Margaret showed me in. Although it had been a year since I last saw the wee lassie, to her it must have been ages for instead of 'hello Uncle West" all she offered me was a shy smile.

"Oh how you've grown Kirsty,"I smiled broadly at her. Kirsty's smile disappeared as quickly as it had appeared. "Daddy said to give you these until he comes home," I lied holding out the little box. "He said those are the mints that you like. Remember I gave you some for your last birthday." Mark having told me, how much she liked them, and strangely I had not forgotten.

Timidly she took the box from me, with a thank you. But minus the Uncle West.

"Daddy is going to be away for a wee while working. He'll probably bring you a better present next time, when he comes home."

Margaret's look said 'I hope so.' She put a hand on her niece's shoulder. "Don't you have homework to do?" she asked softly. A nod from Kirsty said she had. "Then say goodnight to Uncle West."

Kirsty looked up at me. "Good night...Uncle West."

I bent forward and kissed her on the cheek. "Goodnight Kirsty. I'll try to see you more often."

When the door had closed behind the little girl, Margaret slumped into a chair, asking despondently, "I take it there's no news of Mark or the other man?"

"Nothing so far." I sat down across the table from her. "But it's early doors yet."

"Early doors! Mark could be dead for all we know." Her voice rose, bordering on the hysterical. "And if so what will I tell his wee lassie in there!"

I had no real answer or hope to give, yet somehow I believed Mark was still alive.

"There's been no news at all. And if Mr Muir has been abducted, there's no news so far as to what they want. Although I should guess it's money."

Margaret looked puzzled. "Surely it's obvious. Isn't this Mr Muir rich?"

I nodded. "Yes but it could be more complicated that than."

"And what about Mark? Do you really think he is alive?"

I nodded again. "I'm sure he is. There's no reason to think otherwise."

I rose before Margaret could ask any more awkward questions. Questions I knew I couldn't answer. "I'll have to go now, Margaret. I'll call you, if and when I hear anything."

Margaret too rose, "Oh I'm sorry West, I've never offered you a cup of tea," she apologised.

"Maybe next time Margaret, and let's hope I'll come with some good news."

Thankfully the ground was dry when I set off across the open ground. No lights shone in the Muir mansion standing gaunt against a moonless night, and I cautiously approached it from the conservatory at the rear of the building.

For a moment I stood looking around for any sign of life, such as a full squad of cops backed by a couple of tanks waiting for a fool such as myself attempting to break in.

My reasoning with the exception of the tanks was not too absurd as most of the population of Scotland would have known the house to be deserted, its master having mysteriously vanished.

I stood close to the back door turned the key that Livvy had given me, gently pushed it open and stepped inside.

Silence, except for my deep breathing which I was sure could be heard in the nearest village if the wind was in the right direction. I stood listening and waiting. Still nothing, not even the merest sound of a twitching curtain, or a creaking door. Silently I made my way to the ground floor study, knowing the odds of finding anything of importance lying carelessly on Mr Muir's desk was close to zero as anything of significance would most likely be in Bert Thomson's hands by now, or at best in a safe hidden behind any one of the numerous paintings on the wall. So why was I here? The reason was simple, and so was I, but I had to try.

As luck would have it what I came across on the third drawer down on the mogul's desk, was not what I expected. In itself it would have meant nothing had my eye not caught the name on what looked an insignificant sheet of paper.

It was then I heard the first creak, followed by a brief beam of light. Someone else was in the house besides myself. Soft footsteps drew closer. I was almost choking with fear as I shuffled behind the study door. Who was it? Someone else on the prowl? The black arm reaching for the light switch told me that I could not afford to be seen or even briefly recognised. My thoughts cursed for me. Thomson had left a uniformed officer to apprehend someone as foolhardy as myself. This time a little curse escaped me. He was not likely to be on duty alone.

I grabbed the arm and hurled its owner head first against a wall. Then I was out of there not waiting to see the man fall or what other damage I might have caused.

I reached the back door, the sound of the upstairs toilet flushing told me that I was right, one cop was not on his own, another was on the throne. Thomson was not so daft as I had thought, having anticipated that some nosey parker would come snooping around, and he had, me Mr Snoopy himself.

I headed for the trees at the rear of the house, hoping to reach there before someone recognised me by my slight limp. If they did it was all up. Thomson would see to that.

Once there I took a hasty look back. Now the place seemed to be swarming with uniformed officers of the law, Thomson had taken no chances.

A few bushes, although barring my way lent to my concealment. Gasping I made down towards the river, it was well out of my way, but at this juncture well out the way by whatever direction was good enough for me.

It took me the best part of an hour before I came across my car, now grateful that I had left it so far away from the house. I started the engine and despite the coolness of the night I was sweating profusely, adding to which the headlights of a car some distance behind me lit up my own car. Panicking now at the prospect of being caught or at least identified by my number plate I gunned my already protesting vehicle.

I was lucky, switching off my lights the chasing car, believing I was still ahead sped on while I had dodged down a single track lane. Vaguely aware of where I was I drove slowly on without switching my lights back on, eventually emerging on to a secondary road.

With the feel of an even road surface beneath me I switched on my main beam and accelerated down this new road with the lights of Haddington in the distance.

By the time I reached North Berwick I had time to think of my next move. Leaving my car in the car park I quickly made for my office. Locking the door behind me, I climbed the common stair to the corridor and offices above, not turning on any lights until I had safely reached my own office.

Somehow I had the feeling I would not be alone for long, so with this in mind I hastily threw off my jacket, and scattered a few papers on my desk to look as if I had been busy. Next I hurried down the corridor to the communal kitchen and put on the kettle to boil, popping a tea bag into a cup while I waited.

I was right, ten minutes later I heard the downstairs doorbell ring. I switched on my intercom. "Hello, I'm closed until tomorrow. Can your business wait 'till then?"

"No," came the abrupt reply. "It's the police here. Open up please."

"Ok. Down in a second."

I hung up my jacket, rolling up my shirt sleeves on the way to the downstairs door, opening it to a plain clothes officer."What can I do for you officer?" I asked pleasantly, having acknowledged his ID card.

"Can I come in sir," the edge in his tone told me I was already a suspect in what I already knew.

"My office is upstairs. I've just put the kettle on. Would you like a cuppa?"

"No thank you sir," his answer gruff having already found me guilty.

"Well then what can I do for you?" I asked making myself comfortable behind my desk, and sipping by now my ice cold tea.

"Have you been here all evening?" Now there was no polite 'sir'.

"Why what's going on?" I didn't know this man and because of his none too polite demeanour I expected he was a new recruit to Thomson's squad.

"I'll ask the questions, if you don't mind."

The hostility in his voice had risen, so I gave a shrug in order to give myself time to think.

"Normally I lock up around six. Tonight I'm working late as you can see." I waved a hand at my untidy desk.

"Can anyone verify this?" His eyes roaming around the room.

"Yes, mostly those in the other offices who were leaving for home around that time would have seen me making for the kitchen as I passed." What a load of lies I thought to myself

"Mm. And you were here all night?"

"Why, where else do you think I could be with all this work to get through before tomorrow?" I let my voice rise in anger, "which doesn't seem likely with all these daft questions you're having me answer. Why don't you come to the point and tell me what's going on, then maybe I can help you. Or did your boss Thomson send you here just to annoy me?"

At the mention of Bert Thomson, he froze momentarily. "You know?"

"Oh do I know him? My brother Fenton and I had the misfortune of having to work beside him."

The officer swallowed, and I could see his eyes glaze a little at the mention of another superior, in this case one senior to Thomson.

"Very well sir," The sir was back. "I'll inform my superiors that I have spoken to you and you have been here from approximately six o'clock until now." He turned towards the door, then swung back. "I take it you have not gone out at all this evening."

I sighed, giving the impression that I did not know the rationale behind the question. "Where would I go and why, officer?"

"Precisely sir. Sorry to have bothered you. I'll see myself out."

I lifted a sheet of foolscap from my desk and without looking up, I said, "you do that, officer. You just do that."

I had taken the precaution of using a car park a good distance away from my office on the off chance of my recent visitor finding it and by feeling the bonnet would still find it warm.

I had only just arrived home settled down to an egg sandwich with sauce, when my doorbell rang and upon answering found the delightful DC Thomson standing there.

"Oh won't you come in, officer," I invited him with as much sarcasm as I had brown sauce on my sandwich.

Thomson mumbled 'something' under his breath, only I

guessed that the word was not anything like 'something.
"Would you care for a cuppa? I was just about to have one,
having just this minute arrived home from the office."

Thomson's face twitched, and I went on sarcastically.
"However you should know that, since it was your new
man who paid me a visit there a short time ago."

"Let's cut out the crap, Barns." Angrily he went on,
"someone broke into the Muir mansion this evening, and
somehow I have a gut feeling it was you."

"Sure you're gut feeling's not a touch of diarrhoea?"

"I said cut out the crap!" he roared at me.

"It's you that should cut out the crap, it's your gut that's
playing up," I laughed.

My weak joke only added fuel to his anger. "One of my
men saw a car very like yours drive away after they had
chased it through the grounds."

"Like mine officer? Only like mine? Your man's not
positive?" I sat down on the settee making myself
comfortable. "Oh, excuse my manners, please have a seat."
I smiled up at him, happy that I had gotten away without
anyone seeing my registration number. "Besides, any
officer of the law could catch me should they walk fast
enough." I tapped my leg. "Not what it used to be. But
then again you would know that. And my limp gives me
away every time. Sure you'll not wait for a cuppa?"

Instead of accepting my offer Thomson swung for the
door. "Next time Barns, next time."

"I can hardly wait, Bert," I offered him my best smile. "I
can hardly wait.

Despite being dead tired I went over in my head the
name I had seen on the sheet of papers in Muir's desk. It
was Grey and Co. Traders in construction tools. I had
almost choked when I saw it, for this was the same lot that

chased me when I caught them fly-tipping. But why should a mogul such as Muir own a crap lot like this? It was most certainly what was known as a subsidiary Company, or a tax dodge or something like it. I yawned and turned on my side. Tomorrow I would pay Grey and Co a discreet little visit.

After calling on an all but brief visit to Margaret and wee Kirsty, sadly with no news regarding Mark, I left to carry out my little investigation of the fly, fly-tippers.

It was a dull damp October night when I started for the yard of Grey and Co. It was as I drove out of the street where Mark lived that I first spotted the wee red car. Another corner and the car was still there. I accelerated and turned into another street, and halting abruptly just round the corner quickly got out of my car, and nonchalantly leaned on the bonnet, arms folded in what I believed to be a fair imitation of James Bond. The red car screeched to a halt a few feet away from my own. Levering myself off the bonnet I walked the few paces to stare down at the angry face of Livvy glaring hatred up at me.

"What's a nice lady doing in a place like this, pray tell?" I asked jovially, or only partially so, for now I was suspicious of this lady also being involved in her employers and Mark's disappearance.

"I could ask you the same question West Barns," she shot back at me through her open window.

"I am a detective, you know. So what's your excuse?"

Livvy got out of the car. "I thought you might know something about Mark. Where he is…, anything." The last said so quietly that I could scarcely make her out.

"What makes you think that Livvy?"

She shrugged. "Well you two knew one another before

this, and you both shut up when I asked about your being in the police force.”

“Is this all that’s to it? Maybe something a little more?” I teased, but in quite a serious way.

“What do you mean?”

“Come on, Livvy. As I said I am a detective and it wouldn’t take even a bad one to see the way you both look at one another.” Even in the darkness I saw her blush.

“Well we did know one another. That’s how I got the job. I got it through Mark.”

“Did you know, Mr Muir, before you got the job?”

Livvy shook her head. “No. I replaced the old lady who looked after him.”

“I see.”

Livvy looked up the road then back at me. “Where were you headed before you spotted me? Have you got a clue as to where they both are?”

“Not a clue, or only a slight one. There’s a construction yard I want to have a look at.”

“Can I come?” Livvy’s voice was soft, almost pleading. Now she was no longer the hard domestic that I knew at the big house.

I thought for a minute. Perhaps she could act as lookout. Then again perhaps not, for I did not want her involved with the two wasters that I had previously encountered. In fact I did not want to be involved with them either.

She saw me hesitate. “I’ll do whatever you say, West. I won’t get in your way. Cramp your style as they say.”

“Much too late for that lady. My cramps a little more like arthritis now.”

Taking my so called wit as a yes, she smiled gratitude at me. “Thanks West.”

“Don’t thank me until you see what you have let yourself

into. Park your car over there."I pointed across the road. "We'll go in mine just in case we have to make a quick getaway."

I drew up a little distance from the yard of Grey and Co. and started to get out. "I'll leave the car here."

Livvy made to open her door. "No, Livvy you stay here. I don't know what this is all about, nothing, most likely. You get ready to drive out of here like hell if you see me running or should I make that limping fast. Ok?"

"Ok" Livvy sounded none too pleased. "Do you think those over there," she nodded towards the yard, "have anything to do with Mark's disappearance?"

I shrugged. "Who knows, although I very much doubt they are involved in their boss's abduction."

"Their boss's?" she asked puzzled.

"Well our Mr Muir owns the business and maybe those guys as well."

Again she looked at with the same puzzled expression. "You mean Mr Muir of Muir enterprises or whatever the hell it's called, owns a shit little place like that?" Livvy pointed at the windscreen.

"Hard to believe, I know. But he does."

"Whatever for?"

I shrugged again, my hand on the door handle. "As I said, it beats me."

Once out of the car I turned to look down at her through the open window. "Remember, get behind the wheel. The gears will be the same as yours, so no need to cross your legs or anything."

"Smart arse." She glared up at me, then quite softly. "Be careful, West."

"I always am. Cowards are built that way." Giving her a

wink, I started off across the road, to the iron fence surrounding the premises, optimistically trying the padlock on the iron gate, and making a face at its stubbornness to unlock. Unlike movie PI's I didn't own a little wallet with various types of tools for such an occasion.

Next I cautiously made my way around the fence perimeter. The portacabin that I took to be the office was in complete darkness as was the large garage standing by its side, the yard filled with a cluster of various types of construction equipment.

If I hoped that at the rear of the premises I might find a missing iron railing or two, I was mistaken, all that I met was tall grass and a few broken vodka bottles.

For a moment I stood there contemplating whether the effort to climb over the fence with the intention of having a peek in the cabin would be worthwhile, although I did not know what I should find.

I am glad that my contemplating is slow, and always has been, for without warning a Rottweiler came charging and barking at me, thankfully from the other side of the fence, drawing up to give me an unobstructive view of its teeth, not one filling to be seen, at the same time as the entire yard was lit up by a powerful overhead flood light.

The thought that it was time to leave was still forming in my head well after my legs were on their way back to the car, and I could scarcely believe that the swishing sound was bullets flying into the grass around my fleeing feet, while on the other side of the fence the figure of a man accompanied by his frenzied dog had unlocked the front gate, with the Hound of the Baskervilles bounding towards me. Now it was a race back to my car.

Still some distance away from the car I shouted out in a paroxysm of fear "Livvy! Get the car started!" and sucking in my last reserves of strength over those last few strides reached the car, and wrenching the door open hurtled myself into the passenger seat.

"Get going!" I shouted at the empty seat. Livvy was not there!

I was in the midst of struggling to the driver's seat when a breathless Livvy hurled the door open, our bodies meeting somewhere over the gear stick as we made for the accelerator in opposite directions. Livvy won. Outside the dog was snapping and scratching the car door as she took off down the road, passing an angry man that I had the misfortune of having met before at the fly tipping.

"Where the hell did you get to?"I shouted at her, more out of relief than anger.

"I had to pee. When a girl has to go she has to go." she shouted back.

"Went for a pee! That's nothing to what I would have done had that dog got me, "I shouted back, this time a little quieter.

Suddenly we both laughed.

"Is your business always this exciting?" Livvy turned to give me a most enchanting smile, "well something like that?"

"Yes some dog owners who have lost their beloved pets can get pretty nasty if I don't find them before their next walkies."

"You'd not want to find one like that one who almost bent your door with its teeth," Livvy grinned.

"No," I agreed sitting back in my seat and eyeing the road ahead. "Where're we going?" "Your place or mine?" came the unexpected reply.

She saw me smile. "But not for what you think, West Barns."

"Not even for first aide, or maybe counselling after my ordeal? You never know I might require mouth to mouth after that trauma. I'm not as young as I used to be," I replied affecting a sad air.

"And you're not likely to get any older, if you try anything, Mister." Livvy turned into a lit street. "I only meant we could have a drink after…well after what we just went through."

"We?"

"Well. You know what I mean."

"Ok. Let's settle for somewhere in North Berwick. I know a good quiet pub. Suit you?"

"Ok. Let's do that, but we'll have to come back for my car."

"Where do you live? I never got around to ask,"

"East Linton, a nice wee place where residence live a quiet peaceful life."

"Not all of them," I chuckled.

I'll ignore that, West Barns," she grinned. "So where are we going for this important conference?"

"Just follow this road and I'll tell you when to change direction," I instructed her.

We had almost reached Dirleton before Livvy asked hesitantly, "How did Mark come to leave the force?" Almost immediately her body language said she should not have asked, for fear that it was an answer she did not want to hear.

"Perhaps that's something you should ask the man himself."

We sat quietly in the corner of the pub sipping our drinks just as quietly.

Finally Livvy said."Why should they be shooting at you West? Surely not for.."

"Snooping around."

"Will you call the police?"

The serenity of the established was shattered by my unintentionally loud "No! Sorry" I apologised. "That's the last thing I want to do, especially to have DC Thomson asking what the hell I was doing there."

"Does he know about Mr Muir owning the place?" Livvy took a little sip of her drink.

"Probably, by this time. Thomson is a pain in the arse but he does get things done. He will have come across the same papers in the old man's desk drawer as I did."

Livvy drew me a look. "Were you going through your bosses stuff while you were looking after him?"

She looked shocked, so I further shocked her. "No, I did that one night after I was unceremoniously asked to leave the Muir dwelling by our beloved cop."

Livvy threw her eyes to the ceiling. "I don't think I want to hear anymore about that if you don't mind." She let her eyes roam around the few others in the bar sitting quietly talking, to one man alone with only his mobile for company, a faint smile on his face told he was not altogether alone, and I remember the saying you're not alone with a book, now it applied to mobile phones. You're never alone, with a phone, especially if it was riveted to your hand.

"Where do we go from here?" Livvy ran a finger round the rim of her glass.

I liked the 'we' bit, until remembering that pal Mark had first choice.

"Beats me. I haven't a clue what's going on. But there is one thing I do know, and that is that our mutual boss was as close to being bedridden as I am to my first dinner."

Chapter 4

A week had gone past when I got the message inviting me, if that is the correct word to the city morgue, and when I attempted to ask more, was given the answer that it was D I Thomson's instructions and that this was all I was to know at present.

To say the least that I could not get there fast enough was an understatement, all the while throughout the drive wondering who it was that they had found, for it could not be anything else. Or was it both men? And for the hundredth time cursed Thomson for his insensitivity.

Muir meant little to me, though I did not wish him any harm. But should it be Mark? What was I to tell wee Kirsty, and for that matter Margaret?

I didn't know whether to feel glad or sad at the sight of old Muir's grandchildren sitting so forlornly on the other side of the glass partition, momentarily thinking that whoever they had found must be the old man, and my heart sank that they might also have found Mark which is why I was here.

It was not long before I was to find out.

"Didn't expect to see you here, West," Ian Kennedy the pathologist greeted me with a faint smile. He was a man in his late fifties whom I knew when on the force.

"No I didn't expect to be here either."

"Doin' all right are you?" I nodded a yes.

Kennedy drew back the white sheet covering the body on the slab. I held my breath the smell of the place as ever sticking in my nostrils.

"Can you identify this man?" he asked still holding the sheet.

I nodded. "It's Andrew Muir."

"You are sure? There's no doubt in your mind?"

"No doubt," I answered. The relief that it wasn't Mark coursed through me.

"How did he die?" was my next question.

"Diabetic coma." The man's words nondescript, it all being in a day's work.

"How long has he been dead?" I choked back a cough.

"Difficult to say, but I should reckon about a week or so."

"Where was he found?"

"Excuse me sir," the uniformed officer standing by the wall interrupted any further questions that I might ask. "But D I Thomson would like a word," he informed me, quietly opening the door.

Outside, Thomson met me in the corridor. He pointed to a room. Silently I went in and he followed.

Without waiting I took a seat. I was still shaking. Thomson sat himself down behind a desk.

First he looked at the female officer sitting in the corner, notepad at the ready, then back to me.

"So that's our Mr Muir, is it?"

At first I was taken aback by the question and lack of formality, especially from one such as DI Thomson.

"Yes."

"He's the one you and Mark Lauder were hired to look after up at his house?" It was really more a statement than a question.

I nodded. "The same."

Shaking his head at some private joke, Thomson stared at me. "You saw the two kids out there," he jerked a finger towards the corridor, "Would you be surprised should I tell you that they both say that the man on the slab is not their grandfather Andrew Muir? You've been guarding the wrong man, Barns. The man's a phoney, an imposter. Who, as yet we don't know, but it will only be a matter of time before we find out, unless of course you would care to tell us who he really is?"

I knew I must look as stupid as I felt. "Not Andrew Muir?" my mouth dry as my brain.

Thomson's eyes sparkled at my discomfiture. "No, Barns. So what's the game? What are you and Lauder up to, eh? Don't try to tell me you didn't know that man lying there is not Muir. You attended to him every day man. You must have known he was not Muir."

The fact that some of the puzzle was falling into place only lent to a deeper puzzle. Such as if not Muir who? And why?

I recovered sufficiently to stare Thomson in the face. "Neither Mark or myself had ever met Muir before that first day. David Campbell set up the meeting but was unfortunately called away before he could introduce us to him. Unfortunately called away, my arse," I swore at being taken in so easily.

"And the woman, Livvy Shaw?"

I shrugged "Mark gave her the work, same as he did me."

"This gets better Barns. Now there are three of you in it."

"Come on Bert," the using of his first name intentionally to put him off guard, "You don't seriously think I could ever be involved in murder? Do you?"

Staring at a sheet of paper on his desk, Thomson coloured slightly.

"No but for the record. Where were you on the day and night that man on the slab disappeared?"

"About what time?"

"All day and night, Barns."

I sat back in my chair, enlightening him about my morning's work until leaving to follow the fly-tippers, then phoning Mark to say I would be late, only to find upon my arrival at the house that both Mark and old Muir were gone.

Thomson shook his head. "Not much of an alibi is it? One who could vouch for you is missing, the other having already left before you arrived. You see how this could be construed if all three of you were involved."

"I thought you said you didn't believe I was involved in murder?"

"No Barns, not murder, but then you could be, inadvertently."

"You mean a patsy as the Yanks would say?" For a brief moment my thoughts were that this man could be right. After all Mark had known Livvy before this job, but even so what was the motive behind it all? Yet I still had faith in Mark Lauder.

"Of course this will all be cleared up when Mr Campbell returns from the Borders tomorrow. He will undoubtedly tell us who the fake Andrew Muir is and the reason why."

"And when will the real Andrew Muir show up?" I asked flippantly.

"That's none of your business Barns," Thomson threw at me angrily.

I stood up. I had a pain in my leg, and Thomson was another one in the neck and now back to his natural endearing self. "Am I free to go?"

Thomson did not get up. "For the present."

My hand on the door handle I asked, "Where did they find him?"

"Oh I thought you knew already and had no need to

ask." Thomson sneered. "In Mark Lauder's car near Whiteadder Reservoir in the Lammermuirs." Thomson shook his head in anticipation of my next question. "No, there was no sign of Lauder, and unless he walked all the way to Gifford or some other place nearby, he had to have an accomplice. Now you can see my point."

I could very well see Thomson's point. To me Mark had also been abducted, but not as the detective believed driven away by an accomplice. The burning question was Mark still alive? And if so where?

No doubt both the real Mr Muir and Campbell would answer these questions; my only disappointment was Thomson knowing why before I did.

I was not left long in ignorance as to who was the fake Andrew Muir. Summoned by Campbell himself to his own office in town the next day.

Campbell was a man I judged to be in his early forties, a man who was clearly used to being obeyed. This I already guessed from our one and only phone call. He must have, 'nursed his wrath to keep it warm'.

"Take a seat Barns," he barked at me. "So what's this all about?"

"I could ask you the same question," I threw back sitting myself down, but not in the one he expected me to. "Don't you want to see any identification? I could well be another fake, like the one you hired to dupe Mark Lauder and myself."

Campbell's look of anger never altered. "Ok. Let's get to the point. I hired Lauder who in turn hired you and the woman Livvy Shaw, I having already known none of you had met the real Andrew Muir. The reason for the deception was simply to have the Press and our rivals believe that because of the Boss's illness he would not be interested in the Highland project, while we secretly concentrated on the real one in the Borders." Campbell saw my look of scepticism. "You don't believe me?"

I shook my head. "No. What's the real reason? I think I have a right to know, especially since my friend is missing and there's a dead man lying in the morgue."

Campbell's features slackened a little. "The dead man is an old one time actor by the name of Martin Quinn. We chose him because he looked quite like the Boss, and was never likely to win an Oscar, or even any work for that matter. All he had to do was keep to his bed while you lot attended to him and we let the Press know where he was, just to keep our rivals satisfied."

"If this was all that was to the job, why was there any reason for anyone to murder him?"

Campbell seemed to sag a little "I ...we don't know. This was never on our agenda. There could never be any justifiable reason for his death."

"Poor sod. He acted his part well, had us scared shitless at times for fear of us losing our jobs."

At this Campbell gave a flicker of a smile.

My curiosity deepening, I asked, "Was D I Thomson pleased by both your statements? I take it he also interviewed the man Muir himself?"

"He was perfectly satisfied by both our explanations." Campbell clipped.

At my wrinkled brows, Campbell's stare was hostile. "You look puzzled Mr Barns."

"Somewhat." I looked him straight in the face. "How come your Boss is back in the Borders? I thought he was supposed to be keeping a low profile."

"Oh I see." Campbell calmed a little. "Mr Muir stays at a hotel close to our new building site. He of course never actually visits the site. Any problems are discussed at the hotel, where he is known under a different name. Satisfied?"

He didn't wait for my answer but went on, "The officer says Mr Muir can return to his home once they give it the all clear."

I rose. Campbell looked up at me, "We'll send you a cheque Barns. No need for you to be out of pocket, there's no point now in continuing this charade now that the police and Press are involved."

I stared at him, anger in my voice, "Sorry Mr Campbell but there is. My friend Mark Lauder is still missing and it's my intention to see that a certain wee lassie sees her daddy again."

I did not recognise the obviously disguised voice on the phone inviting me to meet him if I wanted to know what had happened to Mark Lauder. The place: a disused barn somewhere beyond Kidlaw and that I should come alone.

To me it smacked of something out of an old Humphrey Bogart movie, and I honestly expected to hear the usual sound of someone on the other end being strangled to death with the final choking words of 'it was 'ugg' before all was quiet.

However I was becoming that little bit edgy at the lack of clues surrounding Mark's disappearance, and despite that little voice inside warning me to keep away I decided to risk it, even if was only for wee Kirsty's sake.

With October coming to an end, the cold and darker nights just beginning, I set off for the rendezvous. Over an hour later after much searching of countless country signposts or so it seemed, my car and I were bumping over a road that had more potholes than road, an experience I would dearly have liked to have avoided, more so in my car's case.

Believing by my instructions that I had reached the appointed spot in this isolated spot, with only a few sheep to welcome me, I drew up at a gate leading to a field in which I took to be the disused barn in question.

Ever cautious I left my still groaning vehicle and crossed the field careful to avoid the flat brown soggy land mines that guarded the old barn. I had not polished my shoes to have them squelching in this lot.

For a moment I stood at the barn door and took a last look round at the open farm land before venturing inside.

The door sagged, hanging by one hinge, and it took both hands and all my strength to pull it slightly open.

I took a hesitant step into the dark void of the interior, only vaguely aware of an object swinging rapidly towards me. I jumped to the side and it hit off the barn door and swung back, and I heard a cry of pain.

Now that my eyes had become accustomed to the dark, I saw an indistinguishable heap lying a few feet away from where I stood, a brick on the end of a rope hanging above it.

"Now you've killed my sister, as well as gramps!"

Recognising the squeaky voice I took a few steps further, and peered down at the moaning heap that was Andrew Muir's granddaughter, Miss Cairngorms herself.

"What the..." I stopped "What's this all about?"

Squeaky helped his sister to her feet. "You could have killed her!"

"What about me? He who casts the first stone, or in this case brick.. prick." I was thinking of the repercussions had that same missile found its mark..mainly on me.

Big sister got shakily to her feet, rubbing the area of her chest.. and that was some area.

"You murdered our gramps, that's why you wouldn't let us see him. He was already dead that night when we called at the house."

So that was it. These two daft kids thought I had killed the old man.

I pointed to some hay bales behind them. "Sit your backsides down there and I will enlighten you as much as I can to what's going on."

For the next ten minutes or so, I attempted to explain all I knew. Of course they were aware that the body they had seen in the morgue was not their grandfather, but to them he was still missing so they had mistakenly put two and two together with the assumption that my presence at the house and refusing to let them see the old man was because I had already killed him.

Again my thoughts were on how important all this must be to Muir not to have told his grandchildren who he was reputed to dote on, that he was alive and well.

"Mr Muir will be in touch with you as soon as he can. I am sure he would have done so by now if he possibly could". This was a little lie, the old bugger should have done so by this time and not put the poor kids through all this.

This appeared to convince them that I was telling the truth.

"You came by car?" was my next question.

"Yes. We left it on a side road quite a long way back," Squeaky said.

"Come on I'll give you a lift if you promise not to chuck another brick at me."

Both looked at me to see if I was serious or not. "Just joking. Now remember, don't do anything until your grandfather contacts you. Ok?"

Two heads nodded, together with a "sorry Mr Barns."

Once again careful not to get my shoes dirty, we headed for my car.

Chapter 5

I saw the change in Livvy. Deeply worried over Mark's disappearance she looked tired and drawn. We sat in the same bar in North Berwick as that night I was chased out of Grey's yard. She saw by my expression that I had no news to give her, good or otherwise.

"He's dead. Mark's dead isn't he?"

"What makes you say that, Livvy?" She jerked at the harsh way I had said it, for I could no longer hide my own anxiety and the prospect of having to tell a nice lady and a little girl that someone they loved would not be coming home.

"They killed that poor man, didn't they? Why would they want to keep Mark alive? After all he could identify them."

" Martin Quinn was a diabetic. He died from lack of insulin. I don't believe they wanted him or Mark dead, just out of the way for a while."

Livvy must have found what I had said encouraging, her face lit up. "So you do think Mark is alive and being kept somewhere? Perhaps until this big shot Muir has completed his deal or whatever he is after. It must be some deal to risk the consequences of kidnapping."

"Could be Livvy, but whatever it is, he and Campbell are up to their necks in it. Though I can't help thinking there's more to it than that,"

"So where do we go from here?"

Again I liked 'the we' bit, so I said. "Martin Quinn was abducted for something he had found out, of this I am sure. Something big enough to have him put out of the way for a time, but in their haste forgot to take his insulin with them. That's why I think who actually did the abductions are a right bunch of amateurs at that kind of game."

"Like that Haddington mob with the yard?"

I lifted my drink. "Yes. They could fit the bill."

Livvy took a sip of her drink and gently sat it on the table staring at it as if suddenly it would topple over and spill out the answer to our problem. "Perhaps we should pay those gentle kind people another visit," she said softly.

"What! Those kind wild animal keeping persons?" I shot out aghast.

Livvy laughed. "Yes, but not in the way you expect."

"What other way is there, except to climb over that fence into Jurassic Park" I exclaimed, now truly alarmed.

"No need. Just drive straight in." She gave me an enchanting smile, which under different circumstances I would have interpreted as inviting. Once again I envied Mark Lauder where ever he may be.

"So you expect to just drive in and say, 'excuse me but could I have my boyfriend back please?"

Livvy laughed. "Something like that."

By her expression I knew she was not kidding, and thinking of the ramifications if she were to carry out such a daft plan, I said seriously, "Thomson will probably have found the documents in old Muir's desk, and have already called there as part of his investigation, and if he had found Mark we would have known by this time."

Livvy wrinkled her brows, and I went on. "But let's say for arguments sake that he hasn't, and you go bursting in, no doubt wielding a frying pan, and you fail to make any impression…on their heads or otherwise, you will only have jeopardised Mark's safety. The result of which will be to move him elsewhere and no doubt you as well."

Livvy stared at her glass on the table, "Well at least I will know where he is and we will be together again."

"But for how long?"

Livvy drew me a look. "But you said you believed it was never their intention to kill either Mark or Martin Quinn."

"Yes. But they might be forced to do so if you were to come that close to finding Mark."

And so saying I hoped that I had done enough to convince her.

I thought it safe enough to leave Livvy on her own for a time, so with this in mind I cleared up a few things in my office while thinking of my next move, which was to keep a night vigil on Greys on the off chance that if in fact they did have Mark hidden away they might decide to move him to a safer location. After the third night I gave up.

Eventually, I got round to visiting Margaret and wee Kirsty. Each day seemed longer worrying if Mark was still alive. It was now well past the time that Mark and I had been employed to look after old Muir, and I could not help but wonder if the decoy had worked. Had the real Muir's plan worked? And what was it really all about.

Should neither Muir or Campbell be responsible for Mark's abduction then who was, or were holding him? And now that the deception was over would he be set free?

I shivered at the same thought I had over and over again, and that was that should Mark have seen his captors it was not likely that they would let him go.

Thomson seemed fully satisfied by the old codger Muir's alibi, though I had to admit that I was curious to meet the man. Where was he now? Down in the Borders? If so I hoped the Press were hounding him to find out the reason for it all.

The door opened to reveal the distraught figure of Margaret standing there. "West! Oh West! I hope you can do something with Kirsty, she will not come out of her room. She has not eaten a thing since yesterday morning and neither will she go to school. I am at my wits end."

Sobbing, Margaret stepped aside. "Livvy's upstairs with her now, but she can't do anything either."

I took a look in the direction of the stairs, wondering without success, what help I could be where two women had failed.

Instead I made for the living room. "A cuppa might help."

"Kirsty's too young to drink tea," Margaret said bewildered by my suggestion.

"Not for Kirsty, Margaret, for me." I rolled my eyes to the ceiling. "I just don't have a clue. The wee lassie hardly knows me now. She is not likely to listen to anything I have to say, when she won't listen to you or Livvy."

"Here, I made a pot to give Livvy a cup before you arrived." She pushed a cup and saucer across the table to me.

I thanked her and poured milk into my cup. "What's brought this on all of a sudden?" I asked, sipping the hot liquid.

Margaret shrugged and sat down opposite me. "She thinks her daddy has gone and left her and doesn't love her anymore." The woman's voice softened. "You know what bairns are like."

I shook my head. "No. Even though I was one myself." I smiled at her.

We both heard footsteps on the stair, and Margaret threw me a hopeful look, which was quickly shattered by Livvy appearing alone.

"Oh hello West, it was you I heard at the door."

I nodded. "Nice to see you, Livvy." I jerked my head in

the direction of the ceiling, "No luck up there?"

Livvy made a face. "Fraid not. See if you can do better. Margaret is at her wits end."

"You can say that again." Margaret handed Livvy a cup of tea. "Can you do something, West."

I could, but not what the woman had in mind; my thought of running away wasn't going to solve anything. I rose. "Well here goes nothing as they say."

I heard sobbing before I had reached Kirsty's bedroom door. For a moment I hesitated, wondering what on earth I could say to help ease the wee lassie's pain.

"Kirsty? Can I come in?" Silence. So I asked again. This time there was a muffled 'yes'.

Kirsty sat propped up in bed clutching a teddy bear when I entered. "Hello Kirsty. Not feeling too good, eh wee girl?"

I squeezed myself into Kirsty's rocking chair. "Livvy says that's a nice dress you've got on."

I hadn't known what else to say, and wished I hadn't, for the wee lassie started to howl.

" My Daddy bought me it." She howled even louder through her tears, and I thought there would be two angry women at the door all too ready to' put the head on me' for upsetting their wee cherub. However no one appeared either to chastise or lend a helping hand.

"What's all this about Kirsty? You know you're upsetting Livvy and Auntie Margaret."

Kirsty's howling subsided to a sob then without warning into a roar of crying, the suddenness of which had me almost off my rocker..or should I say rocking chair.

"It's all right, pet," I tried to calm her down. Tell Uncle West all about it."

Kirsty glared at me though her tears the look clearing

saying, 'So when have you started to be my uncle all of a sudden, big man?'

Choking back a sob Kirsty studied her Teddy bear. "Daddy's gone away. He doesn't love me anymore or he would have phoned Auntie Margaret and she would have let me talk to daddy."

"Now Kirsty, you know that's not true, your daddy has always loved you. And he loves Auntie Margaret as well. He wouldn't go away and leave you both. You know that don't you?"

The tearful head nodded, and I went on. "And you know he likes Livvy too." I didn't want to say Auntie Livvy in case I put my big detective foot in it.

Kirsty sobbed a yes. "But where is my daddy and why does he not come back to see me?"

Wishing I had the answer I sat back and eased a hip into a more comfortable position. This wasn't going to be easy. Silently I cursed. Were neither of those women downstairs coming up to help me? "You see." Kirsty wiped away a tear awaiting my explanation, and I too waited, for as yet I had no explanation. Besides, there was no way of explaining the truth to a wee seven year old.

I had half an idea or more precisely a quarter of one, so I began, at the same time wondering where my idea would lead and hoping not where I believed it would. "You know daddy was a policeman?" Kristy sobbed and gave a nod. "And sometimes you would be asleep when he got home at night. Well that's what he is doing now."

Kirsty's eyes opened wide."Daddy's a policeman?" her happy mood was short. "But why doesn't he phone or come to see me. He did when he was a policeman before."

Cunning wee sod I thought she has me thinking 'get out of that one Uncle West.'

I scratched my head careful not to disturb any sawdust. "Well, you see, daddy is on a very important job to catch the baddies, but he doesn't want the baddies know where he lives, so he has to stay away, for he doesn't want them to hurt you or Auntie Margaret."

Kirsty stopped her sobbing and wiped away a tear, her eyes open wide, waiting for me to continue.

"You're daddy is doing a very important job, Kirsty. And he is very brave too." I halted and sat back as far as my lower regions would allow in the tiny chair. "He might even get a medal."

Now perhaps I had gone too far should Mark return unscathed and medal less?

However I would cross that bridge when I came to it. "Daddy has told me to let you know that he is all right, and was there anything that you might want to tell him."

Pleased by what I had concocted I pushed my luck a little further. "You can write daddy a secret letter and I'll give it to him when I next see him. Is that OK?

Kirsty's eyes gleamed. "Can I do that now, Uncle West?

I pretended to consider. "Perhaps after you have had something to eat. I think daddy would want to know that Aunt Margaret is looking after you alright, and how you are doing at school."

Kirsty pushed herself off her bed. "I think I'm hungry now Uncle West."

I stood up and turned for the door. "Then let's go and get something to eat."

"Uncle West," Kirsty giggled. "Can I have my rocking chair back please."

I put a hand down and felt that I was not indeed off my rocker, for the chair was sticking to my rear end and I very much feared I would have to use a tin opener to get out of this one, or what was more, get out of the jam I might had talked myself into if I was not to produce some wee lassie's daddy.

I did not see Livvy for a day or two, as she worked in a solicitor's office for most afternoons. At present I was not Livvy's flavour of the month, believing that I had given up in finding Mark alive. In exasperation I had contacted Thomson, but he had no news to give me, unless that was, that he did have, but was not willing to share with me; same had applied to Livvy and Margaret when they had also called.

A couple of clients had me tied up for a day or two, but I had managed to look up Creada on Google to find that it was a London based construction company, which had me wondering what Martin Quinn might have to do with them. This had been the name on the foolscap that I had glimpsed before that man had rammed it into the folder. Had he discovered something that may have cost him his life, even if unintentionally? After all he did have a mobile, a mobile that had not been in his room after his abduction.

If my hunch was right it might be to my advantage to pay Creada a visit. There were some things that were better done face to face. Or in some cases two faces to one face. However, once again Livvy thwarted my plans.

Chapter 6

It was a dark dreary November evening I thought, looking out of my office window across the Forth to the Bass Rock, sitting ghost like under a leaden sky. It would rain soon, or even sooner. Any further depression was interrupted by my phone. I picked it up to hear the excited voice of Livvy on the other end.

"West. Glad I caught you. I think I know where Mark is." She went on before I could ask where. "I followed our friends from the yard. They disappeared into some field or other."

"Hold on!" I shouted down the phone. "Where the hell are you?" My imagination was running wild. What was the daft lassie up to now?

"I followed them through the Nungate, and now I am somewhere beyond a sign that said Morham Bank. My car is on a dirt track at the top of a steep hill. West!" Livvy sounded close to hysterics. "They've all of a sudden disappeared. I've left my car in a wee track or other and am looking to where their car might have gone."

"Livvy!" I bellowed down the phone. "Go back to your car and wait for me there. Now. where are you? Calm down and give me directions."

It seemed ages before I believed that I was on the right track so to speak when I thought I had reached roughly the place Livvy had left her car, although by this time it was totally dark. I slowed the car searching every side track on both sides of the road.

Though miles away from any signs of traffic or other signs of life for that matter, I dialled Livvy while still driving. No answer. She had either switched off her phone to prevent the 'baddies' from hearing it, or the trees on either side of the road was the reason for the lack of reception. It was the third reason I hated to think about.

It must have been close on nine o'clock well over an hour since Livvy had called before I located her Mini standing some distance off the road partly obscured by overhanging bushes. I pulled in behind it and got out, shivering in the cold of the night, and smelling the rain in the air.

A quick inspection of Livvy's car told me only that it was locked. No message under the wipers, presumably she expected to contact me by phone. So hoping that she would, torch in hand I crossed the road, shining it on the grass verge and undergrowth.

Nowhere on either side of the road did I come across any sign of a vehicle having left the road. I shivered, cursed and walked down the deserted road swinging my torch from left to right in search of a farm gate. Again nothing; only hedges as far as my limited vision could make out.

By the time I had scoured the road for the third time it had started to rain. Now completely miserable I was on the verge of packing it in, or as a last resort a final look further up the deserted road when I heard the sound of a vehicle from somewhere down the hill. Ever cautious…or cowardly I hurried to where our cars were hidden, only just making it before the headlights of a white van lit up the road ahead. Suddenly there was the sound of the van slowing and then halting.

Now even more cautious I crept to the side of the road in time to see the vehicle crossing a field a little distance away. How the hell did it manage that I thought. Hadn't I searched long and hard on that side of the road with nothing but hedges to be seen? No gate, no gap in hedges for any vehicle to drive through.

With nothing but the rear lights of the van to be seen in the distance I hurried to where I thought the van had entered the field. There, plainly to be seen under my torchlight were the deep wheel marks where it had left the road. But how had it driven to the other side of the hedge? I stepped closer, the feel of damp grass on my trouser legs. I stuck my torch into the hedge and let out a gasp. This hedge was attached to a metal frame; a frame that acted as a gate. This was how the van had crossed into the field.

It took only a short time for me to find the bolt holding the hedge apparatus and edge my way through into the field. Had Livvy found this as well? Or had she been close enough behind whatever vehicle she had been following on foot to see it disappear through this man made hidden gate? And if so where was she now?

I followed where the van had gone on an almost hidden track, the rain heavier, and I cursed at not having taken the time to put on my coat. I hurried on in an effort to heat myself, all the while wondering where the hell I was going and more so where the hell was Livvy.

I trotted through a line of trees, where a little distance on the other side stood two rows of hothouses the kind used for growing tomatoes, lights shining through plastic covers. Was this what Livvy had found? This was a long way from finding Mark. Or again this could be an ideal place to hide him. "I think we'll have to install a turnstile here, this is the second one trying to get in free Charlie The man who spoke came out of the trees, the one beside him holding a shotgun in his hands.

"Is this the shortcut to Dunbar?" I asked cheerily.

"Oh a comedian." The one without the gun stepped closer. "Now we have a double act." He

jerked his head. "The stage is over there funny man."

I started walking in the direction indicated to the hothouses, both men close behind.

A few steps short of a door, the spokesman called me to stop. "We'll have your mobile, if
you don't mind."

I started to act dumb, which was not difficult. "What makes you think I've got one?"

"Everyone has one smart arse, so let's have it" he held out his hand.

Knowing there was nothing to gain by refusing, I dug into my jacket pocket and handed him
my phone "Try not to use it too much, I'm not on the lower tariff."

"Still the funny man." The gunman beside him sounded annoyed, so I decided not to push
my luck.

They walked me through the brightly lit hothouse between rows of what I took to be cannabis plants to a door of a stone building. Here my host invited me to take a step or two inside, which I did rather reluctantly. My first sight was that of Livvy sitting on a metal chair against a stone wall in the empty room, and then to the two men awaiting my 'presence', should that be the right word.

"So it's the council's snoop on fly-tippers if I'm not mistaken." The well dressed man, who had the air of being the boss and closest to Livvy greeted me. "You should have stuck to your day job my friend."

My eyes drifted from the speaker to the heavily built man who had been the one that I had walloped with my camera at the dump site and who looked by the gleam in his eyes that he could not wait to finish our little bout.

"Now thanks to your girlfriend here, you've both seen too much. So what are we going to do with you?"

"I have a suggestion," my former protagonist suggested with a smirk.

I bet you have, I thought. Silently I also cursed Livvy for getting me into this, for there was no way this boss guy was going to let us go. "Set us on our way and we'll not tell anyone the secret of your success in growing tomatoes," I suggested. My quip was not very amusing I knew, but I hoped it would somehow help to lighten the situation in Livvy's case, although by the way she was glaring at the enemy chief it was he who would need the help.

"Sill the comedian," the one with the shotgun said, his tone suggesting he wanted it all done and dusted where Livvy and I were concerned.

"Get young Douglas in here, we don't have much time to get loaded. The leader rapped out his instructions, and advising me on his way to the door, "Grab a seat beside your girlfriend over there." He jerked his head in Livvy's direction, "we'll try not to keep you too long." His laughter followed him into the passageway.

For the briefest of time I felt a little relieved that I was neither to be shot on the spot nor roughed up by my fly tipping friend, this I was sure would come later.

I crossed to Livvy and sat down next to her, patting her hand. "Chin up we'll get out of this somehow," Hoping that the 'somehow' did not mean dead.

"Sorry West it's all my fault I should have waited for you." Livvy turned, her face white. "They can't let us go. Can they?"

I didn't want to state the obvious, so in order to cheer her up and convince myself however unsuccessful that might be, I answered softly. "We're not dead yet." Livvy let out a groan. Well done West you have always had the knack of putting people at their ease.

"Do you think Mark is here somewhere, West?"

I shook my head. "I don't think these guys have anything to do with the Muir affair. I think you have just stumbled into something quite different."

"And much more serious," Livvy said angrily. "So is the Haddington yard just a front for their drug dealings?"

"Yes. I believe the tipping place was where they transacted their business. No one would suspect anyone conducting business in that sort of place. It just so happened that they became that wee bit careless as is often the case with criminals, and I just happened to come across their little game, but I did not know it at the time."

While I spoke, the door opened and two men came into the room, one I guessed to be no older than seventeen or so. The elder took a look across at Livvy and I sitting there then back to the youngster.

"You know how to use this? He handed the boy a pistol which I thought I recognised as a Glock 19 handgun. The boy drew back as if what he had been asked to hold was a snake or at least a dead rodent of some kind.

"I cannae shoot anyone!"

"If it comes to it you better, or you might end up on the wrong end yourself if the boss gets to hear of it. We need you to look after those two." He waved the gun in our direction. "We have to load up the van and be on our way in the next half hour. Don't worry kid, they won't give you any trouble. Now take it." He shoved the gun into the boy's hand. "It's loaded, so all you have to do is pull the trigger. Ok?"

Reluctantly the boy took hold of the gun, something he clearly did not care to handle.

Grinning, his friend opened the door."Just point the

damned thing. It doesn't matter where you hit them, they are dead anyway." He too left the room, laughing. My thoughts were that they thought it was me, who was the comedian.

Beside me I felt rather than saw Livvy stiffen, and I could not blame her.

I studied the distance from where I sat to our young captor standing with his back against the opposite wall, his face a nervous determination not to fall foul of his seniors, and I suspected most of all, his boss.

It was obvious by the way he was holding the gun that he had never been in such a situation, therefore, any sudden move by me could very well result in his shooting wildly in my direction and if not actually succeeding in hitting me or Livvy, maybe doing just as much damage by bringing down some plaster from the ceiling. I wasn't sure which I preferred most, the gun in the hand of an amateur, or a professional who knew what he was doing.

"What are you thinking of doing, West?" Livvy whispered.

"Can't, there's no toilet in here."

Livvy gave my arm a slight punch, clearly having expected more from a hardened ex cop turned detective.

"You could faint, or even pretend to have taken a seizure," I suggested.

"I could give it a try," Livvy murmured. "You say when."

"Whit are you two up to, eh? I'm no stupid ye ken." The boy drew a little closer, and then realising what he had done took a step back.

"So much for that idea," I sighed.

"I've had enough of this." Livvy was on her feet before I could stop her. "Go on then shoot me, you little shit!"

Livvy hurled at the boy

I too rose and took a step to the side. "If we come at you from two different directions, pal you can't hit both of us. And should you hit me and not the lady here, she will kick you where it hurts most. And that's just for starters. She's got a vicious left hook too."

Our young captor took another step backwards, his face twitching his gun shaking. "Don't come any closer," he choked, nervously pointing his gun at Livvy then at myself.

I took a deep breath and drew slowly closer, scared that the frightened kid would let loose at any time.

"Come on then little schoolboy don't tell me you're scared to use that thing." Livvy pointed to the gun.

I gulped. I knew she was trying to distract the boy, but was she going too far? Would he let fly at the insult?

"Schoolboy! I'll gie ye schoolboy!"

I was across the intervening space launching myself at the boy when the gun went off, and at the same time was vaguely aware of Livvy lying on the floor while I grappled for the gun before he fired again, this time point blank at my midriff. Fortunately for me I was the stronger and succeeded in wrenching the gun out of his grasp using it as a hammer on his unprotected curly but thick head, and he slid unconscious against the wall onto the floor.

I swirled around, fearful that Livvy had been hit, hearing her let out a few unladylike curses.

Shakily Livvy rose to her feet. "Must have bloody tripped on something, West," she explained angrily, pushing back a strand of brown hair. She looked to where our recent gunman lay. "Is he…you haven't…"

"No," I assured her. "Let's get out of here before the 'baddies' come back."

Gun in hand I made quickly to the door and pulled at the handle. This time it was my turn to curse, the door was bolted on the outside.

Livvy let out another curse on my behalf. "Sorry West," she apologised. "All this is getting right up my nose."

I could have told her it was her nose that had got us into this mess in the first place, instead I said. "Not to worry, we'll think of something."
"We, West? You don't think I'm used to this sort of thing?"

Now all we could do was wait until the gang came back, and I didn't relish having to shoot it out, more so with the one with the shotgun.

I heard a moan. It came from our young friend who was now tenderly rubbing his head.

"Give him another one, West," Livvy said, quite unsympathetically I thought.

The boy looked up at me through his still dazed state, fearing that I might give him another one for luck and drew himself into a sitting position against the wall.

"Just sit where you are kid and no harm will come to you. Move, and I'll set the lady on you."

"Smart arse." Livvy tried to hide a smile at my so called threat.

The boy moaned and rubbed his head." Did ye have tae hit me sae hard?"

"Hard is yet to come, son." I glared down at him. "You're in trouble. You know that."

"I'm in trouble! Wait till the boss comes back then you'll know who is in trouble."

Livvy took a step closer, and the boy looked as if he was trying to become part of the wall, away from this furiously mad female. "Are you holding anyone else here? She gave his foot a kick. "Someone about his age?" She pointed a thumb at me.

He shook his head. "No. Ouch!" Livvy kicked him again.

"Are you sure?"

The boy rubbed his ankle where the last blow had struck. "I'm sure…I'm sure," he howled.

I came to the boy's rescue. "I think he's telling the truth, Livvy. Mark's not here."

Dejectedly, Livvy threw her hands in the air. "So what do we do now? Wait until his lot come back?"

"And when they do," the boy grinned, now more cheerful at the thought. "Then it will be my turn."

"Don't be too sure." I nodded at him reassuringly. "When we get out of here…and we will, you will be up to your dummy tit in it son. You're up for kidnapping, drug dealing, assault, menace with a deadly weapon, not to mention owning a firearm without a licence."

I threw in the latter in way of a joke, but the boy had taken it seriously.

"I don't own the bloody gun" he hurled at me, his previous confidence gone. "It belongs to Mr Mason."

"Who's Mr Mason when he's at home?" Livvy stepped closer to the boy.

"He's the Boss. It's his gun."

"So he wants you to do the dirty work, Eh?" Livvy made a show of understanding. "Same with all the big men, they get away with it and you take the fall."

There was no time to ask any more before I heard the sound of voices, and I rushed to the door, signalling Livvy to sit back in her chair by the wall.

Fortunately the door swung outwards and the man who had opened it did not expect to have a Glock 19 pistol rammed against his throat, and a voice saying, with as much calmness as possible. "Won't you please step inside gentlemen?"

I grabbed my captor's arm and drew him inside, the gun still at his throat "Tell those behind you not to do anything stupid or this gun might go off."

Luckily for me they complied, shuffling back against the wall their hands in the air.

"Come on Livvy, it's time we left if you want to see your favourite TV programme."

"Still the comedian."

The one who had spoken was the man who had previously held the shotgun, now thankfully without his favourite toy. He swivelled to the boy now standing shakily against the wall. "You let them take your gun? The Boss will have something to say about that. I told him it was the wrong thing to do. You useless little shit," he said scathingly.

"Oh I don't know about that," I chuckled; he's not in any worse mess than you. Time we left, but before we do, how about giving back our phones and car keys." I held out my hand to the man beside the gunman. When he made no attempt to do so, I pointed my weapon at his leg.

The man's eyes said I was bluffing. "You fire that thing and they'll hear it a mile away, and they'll be here to ram that damned phone down your throat."

I could have answered something smart like I don't take inside calls but instead I chose to say, "Not as much noise as you will make when I shoot you in your big feet."

"Or your big mouth, "Livvy added.

I held out my hand. "Give them here,"

Don't have yours… or hers," he said indignantly, "the Boss has them. Quite interesting too. Something about your boy friend being missing," he sniggered at Livvy.

I was anxious now, the longer we delayed the more chance there was of the Boss coming to see what was going on, and I was sure it was not to offer either of us a cup of coffee. So I decided to forego the opportunity to search our adversaries.

Keeping a careful eye on our 'baddies', Livvy and I backed our way to the door, closing and bolting it from the outside.

"First my car keys then my bloody phone!" Livvy swore.

"Come on Livvy," I began to run. "I should have risked the time to search them for their phones."

Livvy ran beside me. " Too late now, but where do we go from here?

"I don't know if we can make it to our cars." I took a hasty look across to where the white van stood, my thoughts on how many of the gang might be there.

At that moment one man started in our direction, which convinced me that he had received a call from our recent captors. And once again I cursed myself for being so thick.

"Look!" Livvy, pulled at my jacket. "Over there!" she pointed towards the house where three men were already running towards where I took the hidden gate to be.

"We won't make it to our cars, Livvy," I gasped whilst running.

I caught her arm and swung her away from the house and towards the woods.

"Where are we going West." Livvy sounded and looked much more fitter than me.

"Don't really know, as long as it's away from the house and those fellows who I suspect will be chasing us at any minute, and hopefully without their canine mutt." I hadn't forgotten the one back at the yard.

The rain was heavier than it had been when I was first captured, and without doubt I'd be soon soaked through.

"I'm up to my ankles in muck, West," Livvy cried out in disgust, drawing up at the first line of trees.

"That's nothing to what you'll be up to if we don't keep going."

My breathing was more rapid than my lady friend's, but fear kept me going. If we were to be caught there could be only one end for us. These guys had too much at stake.

I hadn't a clue where I was leading Livvy but as long as it was away from a line of torches heading in our direction it didn't really matter at this stage of the game. Though it was a pity we were playing the game away from home.

"How many are there?" Livvy asked halting to gain breath.

"I don't know, but I'm sure some will be heading to cut us off thinking we will be making for our cars. We best keep going."

We ran, tripped and splashed through a few puddles in the woods, until finally exhausted drew up.

It was then I heard the sound of a truck it was on a path parallel to where were running, its searchlights lighting up the trees around us.

"Duck!" I shouted and pulled Livvy in behind a tree.

"Where!"

"Not the ones with wings, dafty,"I scolded her.

"Sorry."

For a moment I watched the searchlights sweep in all directions, the truck then moved slowly on.

"We best make away from the road, Livvy. At least their searchlights are telling us where they are."

"And where exactly are we West?" Livvy bent to slip a shoe back into place.

"I don't know, but the further away from here the better"
I led the way. "Although I think if we keep moving in this
direction, we might come close to Gifford."

"I'm sure that's miles away. I didn't drive that far from
Haddington before I left my car to go looking..."

"For trouble." I suggested.

Behind me I heard Livvy quietly swear at my sarcasm.

For the next ten minutes or so we ploughed scrambled
and fought our way through what seemed to be the thickest
undergrowth in auld Scotia, if not the world. Finally we
had to stop to gain our breath if not composure.

Chuckling, Livvy pointed at my face. "You look like
someone in the SAS with black make up on."

"More like a black pudding,"

Livvy chuckled. Serious again she peered through the
trees into the darkness. "If there was only a moon we
might know where we are. Might even glimpse the
Lammermuirs and find our bearings."

I extracted a foot from where it had been cooling off in a
bog. "Bugger." I took a look at my shoe. "Now the bloody
thing's as soaking as my suit."

"Temper, temper," Livvy scolded me. "Like me you
should have come prepared." She showed off her leather
jacket, brown knee high boots and black jeans.

"Show off," I mocked, and once again started to plod
through the East Lothian Amazon.

It was close on an hour later before we halted. Suddenly
and without warning Livvy stopped and threw her hands
up in despair. "That's it! I've had enough. This is
impossible. The whole of Scotland's not this big! We must
be in England!"

"Steady, Livvy" I put a finger to my lips. "I wish we
were!" for only a little distance away sat the truck, its

searchlights sweeping past where we stood. We had run round in a circle!

"Run Livvy! This way!"

"Oh no, more running."

It was at that moment I saw two figures emerge some distance behind us. "Run Livvy! That way!" I jabbed a finger. "I'll catch up. Now run!"

I started off in another direction with the purpose of drawing Livvy's pursuers away from her, and only too well aware that I was unlikely to outrun or lose them amongst the trees I fumbled for the pistol in my pocket. A pistol shot thudded into a tree inches above my head; obviously this gunman had no trouble with his fumbling.

A feeling of déjà vu came over me. Where had this happened to me before? Then I remembered it was a certain little island which was positively a lot warmer than here, except for the situation that was.

I ran but this guy was pretty close behind, too close, and he also had a gun!

I slid down a muddy banking landing up to my knees in dirty brown water, and found that my legs were sucked tight. I turned as best I could and caught the merest glimpse of my attacker a little above me, and before he could take aim I fired, and he toppled down on top of me.

I pushed him away and without a moan or groan he lay there his back against the banking. I had killed him outright.

I had little time to think upon what I done, Livvy was in danger. But where?

At last with a lot of squelching and a lot more swearing I at last 'unsucked' myself, but not before I had to drag the bottom of my little burn, or to the uneducated 'a little stream' with my hands, all the while apprehensive of what

I might grab before my shoe.

With my shoe once again in its rightful place, but rather loose and even more squelchy, I hurried back the way I thought I had had come.

I might never have found Livvy if I had not heard the gunshots, they had come from a little way to my right.

Pistol in hand I hurried to where I believed the shots had come from, cautiously slowing down when I thought I was near. Through the trees stood two men both looking at the body on the ground.

I swore and not too softly for |I was sure the body was that of Livvy.

My anger would have me dash across the intervening space, gun blazing, this, however satisfactory it might be, was not the answer. I had to make sure Livvy was not dead or more to the point badly injured, if the latter, what in the name of hell was I going to do?

I drew to a halt and hid behind a tree waiting to see what my two adversaries would do next.

Almost immediately they slowly walked away talking to one another, although it was too far for me to make out what they were saying. My impatience to find how badly hurt Livvy was, had me clutch my weapon tighter.

Waiting only as long as I thought necessary after the men had gone, I crossed to where Livvy lay, only when I drew closer in the dark did I realise that the body was not Livvy's. Heaving a sigh I scanned around. Where was that woman now?

I heard a slight sound amongst some bushes and held my weapon at the ready.

"Don't shoot! It's me, West!"

"Gone for another pee?" I chided her out of relief at finding her safe.

I walked to meet her, and even in the darkness I saw how pale she looked.

"It's the kid who held us prisoners back there," she said, trembling "They told him he had made too much trouble for them, and although the poor laddie tried to plead that he would do better next time, one said there would be no next time." Livvy spread her hands out in a gesture of despair, her face running with tears. "They just shot him, West. Shot the wee laddie in cold blood. The animals!"

I didn't like to have her think the same would apply to us if we were caught.

Chapter 7

Only a faint glimmer of light showed through the trees above us.

"There! Over there!" Livvy pointed. "Those hills, I think I recognise them"

I followed her pointing finger. "Yip. You could be right. So Gifford should lie in that direction." I nodded and pointed where I thought the town should be.

After another half hour or so of swearing and fighting more undergrowth, we at last emerged through the morning hoar into open farm land.

"Look, a farm!" Livvy cried starting forward.

There, some little distance down a hill stood a farmhouse, a middle aged farmer working by a tractor.

"We've made it, West! We've bloody made it!"

Already Livvy was running and I was following.

"Mister! Mister!" Livvy was calling out while still some distance away, afraid that this apparition in front of her would suddenly disappear.

At the sound of the voice the man swung around, surprise on his bearded face."What the.." was all he got out before Livvy was by his side. "Help us mister there're some bad guys after us."

Relief had me smile at her choice of words and the way she had said them.

The man looked past Livvy to me.

"We got lost. Rambling a bit, got lost last night in the dark."

"Mm.? You best come away in then, you both look fair nithered." He turned and led us into his hallway. "Just go ben there, there's a fire and I'll just put the kettle on. You look as you could baith do wi a cuppa."

"Thanks," I stammered, "but do you have a phone we could use?"

"Aye. Through there. You want to tell your folks you are safe. Is that it? It's on yer way to the fire." He turned slightly. "I will go into the kitchen and put that kettle on to boil."

I hurried the way he had pointed and saw the phone on a little mahogany table, Livvy already heating herself by the fire.

She saw me pick up the phone and smiled. "We made it West. This time I will be pleased to see DC Thomson."

"He might not be on duty but any cop at this stage will do," I assured her.

"Don't think so pal." I swung round to face our host. "Just put the phone down." He motioned that I should do so with the point of his shotgun.

I swore under my breath for again being so stupid. I should have read the signs; no sheepdog, no cattle in the fields, and even by the way this so called farmer had of speaking should have made me suspicious. Now it became clearer, with this guy here owning the land next door to the druggies so to speak it helped to keep any nosey locals at bay regarding the adjacent farmland. I also suspected that our druggies fronted by selling a few tomatoes during the season to any passers- by and locals, just to appear legit. Quite a set up.

The farmer jabbed the gun at us. "Just sit yourselves down in the couch there. OK. And you help yourself to a dram lassie."

Livvy followed his look to a bottle standing on a small fireside table. "A bit early for me," she said scathingly.

"And me. I had a wee one or two while I waited for you baith last night. However ye must have got lost," he chuckled.

I backed towards the fireplace, while the farmer, now gunman lifted the phone, laying the receiver on to the table with one hand, and dialling while covering us with the other.

Although this was when he might be most vulnerable, the distance between us was too great for me to make a dive at him, so the only thing I could do was to stand there and watch him call up his druggie friends, our late pursuers, and await their arrival.

"What are we to do West? Surely we can't get caught now, not after all we've been through?"

I caught the despondency in Livvy's voice while to the contrary our host boasted of our capture to whoever was on the other end of the phone, ending with a chuckle of, "I'll keep the two hares here until you arrive."

Our 'farmer Giles' put the phone down, and still chuckling at his great achievement stepped into the room.

"So you decided not to.."

It was as far as he got before the whisky bottle caught him in the throat, Livvy having caught the man off guard with the speed and accuracy of her throw. Me also, I had to admit, but not so slow as have me more than halfway across the room and grappling with the shotgun before he had fully recovered from his surprise.

Farmer Giles went backwards under my assault, recovering swiftly enough to swing the gun round to a firing position, giving me no time to experience fear that it could go off at any moment, and I could finish up as additional plaster on the ceiling.

Now adrenaline was rushing through me as well as the thought of what fate would await Livvy should I fail, and I

followed up my anger by using a few tricks, none of which
I was particularly proud of, finally succeeding in
wrenching the damned thing from his grasp and hitting
him across the jaw and knocking him backwards to the
floor.

"Livvy !" I shouted. "Get the phone! I'll watch this one.
And well done."

Livvy stepped quickly over our mutual enemy who was
now coming round, and hurried to the phone in the
hallway.

I took a step back and glanced out of the window. So far
so good, but Mr Mason and Co, would not be too far away.
I would dearly have liked a swig of Livvy's 'missile' that
had remained unbroken, which was more than I cared to
think of farmer Giles's jaw, but I couldn't risk it.

"Where are we, West? They're asking where we are
calling from. What's the name of this farm?" Livvy
stamped her feet in frustration.

I confessed I did not know the answer to the latter, only
that a range of hills had been visible in the distance when
we came upon the farm.

At the same time as Livvy was impatiently awaiting my
answer, a four by four had screeched to halt.

"Never mind Livvy, come on it's time we were out of
here."

I grabbed her arm and gave her a push. "Out the back
way, wherever that is," I hurled at her.

"I don't know if I got through or not!" she shouted at me
despairingly.

"Keep running, woman," I called at her back.

"Oh no! More running."

I helped her on her way. "'Fraid so. That way." I pointed
to a door to our right.

Outside we ran across an open field heading for a wire fence bordering a line of trees.

"That way," I puffed. "Get in amongst the trees before we're seen."

Luckily it was not a barbed wire fence, so we easily made our way over it.

I took a step in amongst the trees then turned to look back across the field to the farmhouse.

"Why are you waiting, West? Let's get out of here." Livvy sounded frightened,

"Just to see which way they will come after us. It might give us an edge."

At the same time that I had spoken the four by four took off.

"Where do you think they're headed, West?"

"Could be Gifford. They'll think that's our nearest place. They might just halt and wait for us belting it down the road to the town."

"Belting it!" Livvy drew in a deep breath. "I don't think I've got a belt left in me." She held out the back of her hand for me to see. "Look! I'm shaking all over. And it's not just from cold and hunger."

"Then you should not have been so keen to throw away good whisky." I said tongue in cheek knowing how close the girl was to breaking point. And who could blame her? Before all this, she had simply been a working girl with a boyfriend called Mark, since then no boyfriend, only deaths and mystery, or something to this effect.

"Do you think you got through to Fettes on the phone?" I asked rubbing some circulation into my arms.

Livvy shrugged. "I don't know. I got as far as saying who I was, but when the operator asked the nature of my call and where I was calling from you shouted it was time to leave." Livvy stared at me accusingly. "You grabbed my arm and rushed me down that hallway."

"So I did." I stared in the direction of the farmhouse.

"You're not very observant for a detective, Mr West Barns," Livvy chastised me.

"You observed that did you?"

I took a step back into the trees. "Well observe that." I pointed to the farmhouse where a figure was approaching in our direction.

"More running," Livvy moaned.

"Not if we're quick enough and we head where they'll least expect us."

"This way. We'll skirt the house and head back the way we came."

When well away on the farther side of the farmhouse we drew up to rest. Livvy sat herself down on a large bolder, and I stood sentry.

"Do you think that farmer will have told them whether I got through on the phone or not? I thought I saw him try to get to his feet when we started to run down his hall."

I made a face. "I thought I had knocked him unconscious, but even so, he'll have a wee bit trouble talking for I'm sure I broke his jaw."

"Let's hope we don't bump into him again," Livvy tidied her jacket. "or any of them for that matter," she added with a scowl.

"We best be on our way. Come on girl, let's move it."

"To where?" Livvy rose.

"Back to cannabis land."

Livvy stared at me through those big brown eyes of her, eyes that asked if I was daft.

"I have a plan, just in case our cop friends did not

understand your message."

Livvy threw me a look but said nothing. She did not have to it was all in the look.

The wet weather made it darker than it should have been at that time of the morning. Up ahead stood the hothouses with the big grey stone house to the right.

I drew Livvy back before she had time to step out into the open. "I don't see anyone around."

"They'll probably be down at the farmhouse asking our farmer friend if I got through to the cops or not." Livvy suggested.

"I hope so, for as neither you nor I smoke I need some matches or something for what I have in mind."

"You're not going to..?" Livvy nodded towards the hothouses.

"Oh yes I am." I said in my best pantomime voice.

"Oh no you're not," Livvy answered in the same tone. "You'll get yourself killed should there be some of that gang still around."

"That's why I want you to keep a lookout while I nosey around the house. If setting fire to those plants doesn't bring the cops, it should at least attract the attention of the fire brigade. Don't you think?"

"If you say so, West. Though all I want is to get safely home and into something clean and dry. Don't you?"

"Sure. But I don't think any of your clothes will fit me."

Livvy shook her head in exasperation. "Okay off you go then and be careful. If I see anyone I'll run and tell you."

The house felt creepily quiet when I let myself in by the back door. For a moment I stood and listened for any hint that I might not be alone before I moved to the dining room, the place smelling of stale cigarette smoke and beer.

On the table lay the remains of what looked like bacon and eggs, probably the interrupted meal when farmer Giles' had phoned to inform the gang of our capture.

I scanned around for the elusive matches. There had to be some with all those cigarette stubs in the ashtray. None! I pulled out a few drawers with the same result. It was when I tripped over a rug and stuck out my hand to steady myself on a set of drawers that I saw what appeared to be Livvy's and my own set of mobile phones, and car keys.

My hands shaking, all thoughts forgotten that someone could be in the house I dialled Fettes.

This time I knew the name of the farm and with any luck they would too, even if they had to ask the local constabulary.

I hurried to the kitchen and there found my elusive box of matches. Eureka!

Now to start what I had in mind, and throwing caution to the wind I headed to where I had left Livvy.

"Come on," I called out, running past her. "They've all gone."

"You hope," Livvy replied catching up.

Even so I still kept a sharp lookout on the off chance Mr Big had left a guard or two behind, although I thought his first priority would be to keep Livvy and myself from escaping to tell the world…or at least most of East Lothian about their most exotic holiday resort.

I pulled back the door of the first hothouse and together with Livvy stepped quickly inside.

"How do we start West? I've never started a fire before, especially not this sort." She looked around her at a loss as what to do.

She was not long left wondering, having found a full

petrol can to feed the generator, my first 'batch' went up with my first 'match'.

"Gees it's not long in taking off! This is the warmest I've been all day!" Livvy exclaimed following me down the first row. I swung round handing her a lighted paper taper. "You start the second row over there. Then let's get the hell out of here before we become toast."

"What about the other house?" Livvy followed me.

"One will do to attract the attention of the fire brigade, especially when we give them a buzz."

A few minutes later we stood by the grass verge surveying our handy work.

"Who do you think will arrive first, West, the baddies or the fire brigade?"

I took hold of her arm and swiftly guided her into the trees.

"No matter which, for the moment let's just keep a low profile."

I handed her her mobile and keys.

"Oh you wonderful man!" Livvy leaned forward and kissed me.

"My all that for keys. What would I have gotten if it had been your car that was stolen? I also got through to the law." I stuck my chin up in the air, feigning aloofness. "Being observant I informed them the name of this farm."

Livvy's face seemed to relax, lose all of its tension. "Then should we not make for our cars and get the hell out of here?" she almost danced with relief. "Come on West, you've done enough, let the good guys do the rest."

What she said had made sense, but I was not quite ready to quit. I wanted to see those buggers caught. These were folk who could poison and kill those too hooked to lead a normal life. "You can if you want to. In fact it would be better if you did, then I would know you are safe. You've been through enough Livvy. Go on. We can keep in touch now that we have our mobiles back."

Livvy nodded and turned round, then back again. "No West I think I should like to see the fun."

"Fun?"

She corrected herself, "we'll see it through."

"OK, but let's keep out of sight here amongst the trees."

Just then Mason's big black car roared up the main driveway, screeching to a halt by the front door, the man himself quickly disappearing inside while two of his henchmen ran towards the burning hothouse.

"They'll never put that out," Livvy chuckled watching the men running around for something to quell the blaze.

Agreeing, I switched my attention back to the house. It was too far and too dangerous for me to tackle Mr Big on the off chance he might not be alone. It was just as well that I had, for at that moment a big clanking fire engine sped towards the fire, almost on its tail the white truck veering off in the direction of the house.

Without a sideways glance the firemen unaware of the number of criminals they had at the mercy of their hoses set to work on the fire.

"Can't we do something, West? Mason and his gang are all set to bugger off now that their little game is up."

I shook my head. "Let's leave that to the drug squad. The locals too should be here shortly I should think."

I was right, blue lights flashing, sirens blaring the first of two police cars arrived, one heading for the hothouse, the other for the house itself.

"Do they know Mason and his lot are armed?" Livvy sounded concerned for the policemen.

"I told them that they were," I said above the noise of the fire fighters, my eyes still on the big house.

"Good!" Livvy stamped her feet in excitement. "Here come the cavalry!"

Now there were a further two police cars in the driveway, spilling out uniformed men.

Somehow amid the sound of gunfire the driver of the truck had reached his vehicle, on his heels the unmistakable figure of Mason the boss.

"They're going to get away West!" Livvy exploded with anger.

She was right but there was nothing I could do about it, not at this distance. The black car had also started to move but was quickly brought to a halt amongst further gunshots.

As if by magic, except for the sound of the truck speeding off, there was a sudden silence around the house. In the distance the roar of the fire and exploding glass the only sound.

Then again the roar of cars taking off, this time police in hot pursuit of the white truck.

A full ten minutes later another police car, a little less urgent than the others made an appearance and the unmistakable figure of D I Thomson alighted.

I turned, scoffing. "It's all under control now Livvy, the master has arrived."

"Aren't you going to meet him... them... tell them what really happened?"

"Probably. But right now all I want is a shower a good meal, a warm bed, and not necessary in that order."

Livvy looked puzzled.

"They'll want to interview us soon enough and for me tomorrow will be soon enough. If we go across there now," I nodded towards the house, "Thomson for one will keep us there for hours. At the moment I am tired and soaking to the skin."

"You don't think you could keep your cool is that it?"

Although there was no pun intended in Livvy's question, I could not help myself from laughing.

"Keep my cool? I'm bloody freezing, Livvy." I took her arm ushering her towards where hopefully our cars were still parked. "Get home and do all you have to do to relax and recover. Thomson will contact you soon enough, you'll need all your strength and willpower to keep your cool."

And with that we headed for our cars.

Chapter 8

Next morning Livvy and I received calls from our friends in blue requesting our presence.

We drove there in my car, my hope being that Thomson; for I didn't think it would be anyone else, would not detain Livvy too long, so there was the slightest chance that he might release me at the same time.

Walking down the corridor to Thomson's office, Livvy took my hand. "I wouldn't feel so bad if this was in any way connected to finding Mark, but as it is what will this moron want other than a statement?"

I squeezed her hand tight. "Leave the talking to me. Only answer the questions put to you. Ok? And we might get out of here before we reach Pension Age."

Fortunately for us our mutual friend decided to interview us together, but not in the way I for one had expected.

"So it's you two again." Thomson invited us to sit down. "Now let me get this clear before I take your statements."

He sat there, his look travelling to each of us in turn, then back to Livvy. "It was you who first found this hideout at High Moss, am I correct?"

Livvy looked at me for guidance, after all, had I not said I should do the talking? "It's ok Livvy, tell the man how you came to do his work for him."

Awaiting Livvy's answer, Thomson stifled a retort, and I sat back while she related how she had followed the van from Grey's yard in Haddington, until caught.

Thomson gave a 'mumf', then looked at me to continue, which I did, omitting nothing including my shooting of my pursuer, and the death of the young lad.

When I had finished, the detective sat back in his chair winding his pencil through his fingers. "You expect me to

believe this cock and bull story? Expect me to believe that
Mark Lauder does not play a part on all this?" He threw
his pencil down on the desk and stood up, squeezing past a
female officer taking notes, to stand glaring down at me.
"You see," he smirked "it is too much of a coincidence
that you three should be involved in this drug dealing with
this guy Mason, who would you believe we have just
apprehended."

"Did you get all of them?" Livvy asked.

Annoyed by the interruption Thomson replied angrily,
"No but we will, including your boyfriend."

"My boyfriend!" Livvy was on her feet. "What the hell
has Mark got to do with this?"

I too was curious to know where this was leading, and
for a moment I felt a tightening of my stomach muscles.
Surely I could not be wrong? Surely Mark was not mixed
up in this? But if he was he was nowhere near High Moss
when all this was happening, of this I was certain.

"How do you come to this conclusion, DC?" I heard the
weakness in my voice when asking the question.

"How do I know?" Gloating, Thomson returned to his
chair and sat down "We caught Mason late last night,
although his henchman somehow managed to escape."

"Careless careless," I teased.

Thomson's look was withering. "Only it wasn't Mason
that we actually caught but someone by the name of
Johnny Webster." Thomson stared at me. "You remember
Johnny Webster, don't you West?"

Livvy swung round. "Who the hell's Johnny Webster for
God's sake?" she exploded.

Thomson grinned. "Didn't your accomplice here tell you
about Webster and your boyfriend, how he was the one
and the same who got him thrown off the Force? And you

expect me to believe this is not a coincidence you four all being together?"

"It was West and I who told you about the farm for God's sake," Livvy shouted across the desk at Thomson. "If we were in cahoots with this... this Mason... Webster, why would we bother to tell you where to find the damned place?"

Facing Livvy, Thomson's stare never faltered. "Perhaps a falling out amongst thieves, or a change of sides before things got out of hand and we nabbed you three for complicity to commit murder?"

"What murder?" I asked now angry at Thomson's deductions.

Thomson turned slowly to answer me. "Have you forgotten a certain wee man by the name of Martin Quinn?"

"What's Martin Quinn got to do with drug running, except of course should it be that our esteemed but mysterious Andrew Muir not to mention Campbell his managing director who are behind it all."

Thomson answered as one who held all the trump cards. "While all this was going on Mr Muir has been in America working on the real reason for all this subterfuge. You see with the present project in the Borders not quite complete, he, or should I say his company do not have the resources to finance the present considerably larger one in America."

Thomson saw that I was not completely convinced.

"Now that the cat is out the bag so to speak there is no harm in telling you that Muir also wants the lion's share of a new West Highland project and so to mislead and delay his rivals…"

"Set up Martin Quinn." I completed the sentence for him

"He is as much to blame as whoever killed the poor wee

man," Livvy broke in angrily.

"So why was it necessary to have the actor killed? Isn't that a bit drastic even for rival companies?" I asked.

Thomson gave me a look bordering on hatred. "I thought you and your accomplices could answer that one Barns."

I threw my hands in the air in exasperation. "You aren't still on about that, Thomson?"

The angry detective sat back in his chair. "You have a better explanation?"

"Only that I believe Quinn's death, although an accident was the result of him having found out something about Muir's real reason for having him act as his double. Perhaps Muir was confronted with this, and had Quinn hidden away until this USA project was completed. Muir's being in America at the time does not rule out the possibility of him having someone do his dirty work for him."

Thomson raised an eyebrow. "Like Johnny Webster? "

"Yes, Webster, but not Mark, West or myself," Livvy retorted.

"If only I could believe you," Thomson said, now a little calmer.

I seized the opportunity. I stood up. "Well if that's all, either charge us our let us go."

If Thomson thought he could get away with it he would have strangled me there and then.

Looking up at me from behind his desk, he said, his voice scarcely above a murmur, "Not before you both make an official statement. Then you are free to leave, but only for now. You Barns could be charged with being in possession of a firearm and the killing of a person, unknown at present."

"You'll never make that stick, Thomson, and well you

know it."

Livvy got up. "Since we are to be released after our statements, perhaps your time would be better spent, DC Thomson, in catching those who are holding Mark Lauder, don't you think?"

I was still quietly laughing at Livvy's parting jibe when we left the office.

In the car on our way to our respective homes, Livvy asked."Will you tell me the reason for Mark's leaving the Force?" I noted her use of the word 'leaving' instead of 'being thrown off.' "And what this guy Mason or Webster has to do with it? Please West. I have to know."

She sounded so distraught, and besides she had a right to know. So I began.

"Mark and I worked the same patch and got to know one another fairly well." I shifted into top gear. "Sheila, Mark's wife had just passed away." I turned to look at Livvy, explaining "The big C"

Livvy nodded. "Mark told me that part. It must have been difficult bringing up a kid, Kirsty's age without a mum, although he said he could not have done it without Margaret."

"Yes. Margaret was..still is wonderful,"I went on, "One night Mark was at a party doing some undercover work when who should be there none other than Johnny Webster, who, would you believe had been in the same school as Mark although a few years his senior. Well you can imagine what happened then. Webster didn't blow Mark's cover and for good reason. A few nights later following a tip off about a break-in in a jewellery store, Mark, observed a car flying past at break neck speed and crash into a shop window. Instinctively his reaction was to run to the car to see if anyone was injured, and while he was in the act of helping…a drunk driver by the way, Webster shot past having just finished knocking over the jewellery store that Mark was supposed to be guarding."

"And?" Livvy asked eagerly.

"Webster was caught. He had always hated Mark for one reason or another, and this was his chance to get even. In his statement he declared that he had arranged with Mark at the night of the party what was going down, and had cut him in on the deal, to turn a blind eye. So when the car had crashed it had appeared to look as if Mark had intentionally left his post in order to give Webster a free getaway."

"But surely it was a gangster' s word against Mark's?" Livvy wrinkled her brows unable to understand.

I nodded "It would have been except the cunning bugger had arranged to have £2000 deposited into Mark's bank account for the so called pay off, which although not exactly clinching it, did have the result of having poor Mark having to take early retirement."

"Doesn't add up, surely you can see that West? I mean, how could Webster know about Mark's account?"

I could see a look of apprehension on Livvy's face as she tried to cling to her belief in Mark.

"I have an idea that Webster broke into Mark's house and got the details he needed, there was no sign of a break in but when I see Mark I'll ask him if that could be a possibility"

"Surely he would've noticed?" Livvy protested, always on Marks side.

"Not necessarily, remember he was going through a traumatic time"

Livvy pursed her lips and nodded. After a moments thought she asked "Why didn't the police check up on the account, I mean … where the money came from?"

I looked straight at her, "Mark told me it was a cash payment put in through the night safe at the bank. He even tried for CCTV footage but with no luck"

"Could that be an angle you would look at?" Livvy asked, "I would West, but I don't have the clout you have"

I felt like I could clout someone for not checking it out properly at the time. Still, it could mean I might find out who was responsible and used it as the reason Mark had to leave the police.

I had arranged to pick up Livvy next morning with the intention of paying a visit to Mr Muir's construction site in the Borders. However, fate and a nasty one at that dealt me a cruel blow, but more so Livvy.

It was about ten in the morning and I had just reached my front door when the phone in my hallway rang. Cursing, I turned and hurried to answer it, half my thoughts that Livvy may have cancelled her trip which I thought most unlikely, the voice on the other end quickly dispelled these same thoughts.

"Morning comedian," the voice began softly. "I have your little sweetheart here. So I will make this quick. If you want to see her again all in one piece you had better cough up ten grand."

At once I knew who was threatening me. It was none other than the one with the shotgun I believed was called Charlie.

"I couldn't cough up that amount even if I had bronchitis," I shot back, my mind racing. But how the hell? Obviously he had found out where she lived.

"That's your problem. Now listen and I'll give you instructions when and where to have the money left."

There was no way I could trace the call but I had to keep him talking while my brain, little as it may be, thought out a rescue plan. "Don't try the old trick of having me run from phone box or place to place like some demented eejit, my leg won't stand up to it for a start. So it's one place or none at all."

"Listen motor mouth, I'm calling the shots. Do you want your lover sent to you piece by piece?"

"You wouldn't do that, you couldn't afford the postage for a start."

"Still the comedian. Well here's something to laugh about. Have the money ready by three this afternoon. I'll phone closer to the time with further instructions. Don't involve the cops, or it will be me who has the last laugh doing in your girl friend."

"Three o'clock! The chancellor himself couldn't come up with that amount by that time."

"Lucky you're not the chancellor then, eh. Three o'clock wise guy, now start laughing."

There was no way that I could raise this sort of money in such a short time, and even if I could, I didn't think that by doing so it would save Livvy no matter how concerned I may be over her safety. Still, I had five hours to think up a plan.

By three o'clock I had not heard from my esteemed kidnapper, and I began to worry. All sorts, and I do not mean the liquorice kind began to run through my mind. Such as had he abandoned his idea of holding Livvy to ransom and instead settled to make a run for it?

Somehow I thought not. Evidently he needed the money for a clean getaway as there was no other reason for him taking such a chance. Or was it because he was already mixed up in a killing?

My much awaited call came at 3.17pm.

"You got the money big mouth?"

"And hello to you too," I answered more calmly than I felt. "No I haven't, and I told you as much when you phoned before."

There followed a silence which seemed to last for ages, and I guessed my answer had surprised him. When he did reply it was as though he was attempting to hide his confusion as what to do next.

"Okay, I'll give you till tomorrow evening, nine sharp. No police do you hear? Wait at home for your instructions."

I moved the phone away and heaved a sigh of relief. He had taken the bait and had truly believed I was genuinely attempting to raise the money. I brought the phone back. "Is Livvy all right? Can I speak to her? After all I have only your word that you have her."

"She's all right laughing boy, but just in case you have brought in the cops I don't intend extending this call. Should you not come up with the goods you will hear her... screams and all." At this the phone went dead.

It was a longer day than D-day for me. Several times I thought my watch had stopped, or at least moved backwards. Had I done the right thing? Had I jeopardised Livvy's safety in holding back the money for her release? All these thoughts and more flashed through my rapidly becoming numb brain.

At last the phone rang and although I had sat beside it I almost hit the ceiling.

"Got the money?" the voice said.

"Yes."

"Good. Make for Dunbar, a little way short of the

roundabout there's a track to your left, take it and drive about a hundred yards, stop but don't turn your car around. Got it? Wait there until I arrive. I will halt just inside the entrance. First I will turn my car round, then me and the lady will get out, when you see this, walk towards us until you come to a big boulder. This is where you will leave the money."

"Then what?"

"I pick up the money, you pick up your woman. That's all there is to it pal. Be there by ten. Okay?" he rang off.

I was at the appointed place by 9.15. I sat there in my car looking into my rear and side mirror for any sign of a car, earnestly hoping that it would be the one with Livvy and not some locals out for a joy ride or a couple there to make out. If things could go a 'Rabbie Burns, of mice and men,' it took little imagination to know who was the mouse.

Ten o'clock came and went, with no sign of a car. Was this ned fooling me around? Would I return home to another set of instructions?

It began to snow, little floating flakes at first, but enough to block my rear window. I turned on the wipers just as the headlights of a car appeared at the entrance to the track.

I breathed deeply and got out of the car shivering in a cold blast of wind.

As yet there was no movement from the far away car. Suddenly the lights went off and the driver's door opened.

Charlie had Livvy by the arm his other gripping his pistol. All this I could see through the snow from where I stood, my hand inside my open car door.

They reached the boulder where I had left the money, now the next few minutes were crucial.

For the occasion I had chosen an old holdall that had a

stiff zip. Should my friend decide to stop to make sure that the money was indeed in the bag he would have to release his hold on Livvy, and in doing so give me the opportunity I hoped for while his full attention was on struggling to open the bag. However, there was always the possibility of him having Livvy do this for him and should this be the case and he realised that only the top layer of money was genuine and the rest made up of paper cuttings I, or should I say Livvy, was in trouble.

Charlie looked to ensure I was still by my car, reached the boulder and gave Livvy a push in my direction. He stooped and picked up the holdall and took a few steps back before turning to quickly retrace his steps to his car.

Realising she was free Livvy ran towards me. I cursed and waved her to run to the side. For a moment she kept on running, until understanding what I meant, ran off the path on to the snow covered grass verge, by which time I had the telescopic sight of my rifle pressed against my shoulder, I fired and 'Charlie Shotgun' fell.

I hurried to meet Livvy.

"You've shot him West!"

Without saying anything I walked past her to the boulder, and lifted my holdall, stuffing my banknotes in my overcoat pocket.

Livvy came to confront me."Aren't you tampering with the evidence as they say, West?"

"Only with what's mine. Besides I hope the cops are satisfied with finding Charlie as part of the gang they are looking for, and without any evidence lying around so to speak. Who is to know that I am involved, or that you were ever kidnapped." I walked the few steps to where Charlie lay.

"Have you killed him?" Livvy asked anxiously at my

shoulder.

"No." I stooped and pulled out the dart from the back of his neck. "He's only stunned."

"So am I West Barns. I never know what you're going to do next."

"I know," I agreed, "that's what all the lassies say. Here take my coat you look frozen." She put it on without protest and I handed her my car keys. "Would you mind bringing my car down here, I don't want to hang around in this snow after our friends of the law appear."

I searched through Charlie's pockets and found his mobile. This will do me nicely, I thought.

By the time I had pressed a few numbers on Charlie's phone, Livvy had returned with my car, and I threw my holdall and rifle into the back seat.

Shortly after, when we were well on our way on the A1, I saw the flashing blue lights of the first of the police cars on their way.

"Do they know it was you who phoned them, West?"

"No, I used Charlie's phone. Legally I should have waited at the scene of the crime so to speak, and no doubt be charged with owning and discharging a firearm with the intention…"

"Enough West, please." Livvy pleaded. So I did not mention that she as the victim would also be required to be examined by a police doctor, should we have to explain our reason for being there. Another charge against me. But right now my priority had been to rescue the lovely girl next to me, also finding Mark was more important than finding myself charged or detained by my enthusiastic friendly DC or other 'bobbies'. I sighed and switched on the car heater.

"You'll not get me to East Linton from here," Livvy said alarmed.

"I'm not taking you home, I'm taking you to my place."

Livvy's look dared me to take advantage of her or her situation.

"Look, you need someone to cook you a hot meal."

"I can do that for myself thank you very much." Livvy sounded indignant at my proposal.

I kept on driving through the ensuing silence. Out of the corner of my eye I saw Livvy's head nod a little. Perhaps she had resigned herself to my better suggestion I flattered myself, or she was too tired to object. In a few minutes she was slumped back in her seat fast asleep.

Livvy awoke as I drew up outside of my flat. She yawned and bleary eyed stared around her.

"We're here. Soon have you out of those wet clothes."

"Not on your life Barns," she retorted.

Now it was my turn to be annoyed." I only meant into something warmer."

"So you've done this sort of thing before. You have a range of women's' clothing handy just for such an occasion."

I decided I had to defuse the situation. "You know that's not what I meant. But I will have my coat back pronto if you please."

"Why?"

"Because it's worth a few hundred to me."

Livvy ran a finger over the lapel. "Doesn't seem that much to me."

"It does to me, there's your kidnap money in the pockets."

Unexpectedly, Livvy laughed aloud. Perhaps it was a release of tension, I don't know. I leaned over her and opened the passenger door. "Come on, let's get some food into you."

I thought how pale and tired she looked sitting there in my lounge when I returned from my bedroom. "Here," I threw the PJ's to her "an old aunt gave me these for Christmas. I've never worn them so they are quite new."

I pointed to a door, to her right. "The bathroom's in there. You can shower while I fix us, something to eat."

I'm not the best cook in the world, and have difficulty in using egg cups without instructions but I did my best without the benefit of having watched all those TV cookery programmes and somehow managed to come up with a reasonable cheese and tomato omelette.

The bathroom door opened and Livvy emerged in my PJ's, towelling her hair.

"Feel much better now?" I tried hard not to stare at this lovely lady, wishing I had seen her before Mark Lauder.

"Yes thanks." She sat down at the table.

I placed the omelette before her. "I hope you enjoy it."

"I'm sure I will. But then one will eat anything when one is starving."

Although she had made it sound like a joke I knew she was serious.

I poured out the coffee and pushed the cup across the table to her. "He didn't do anything...Charlie Shotgun I mean." I halted not knowing how to put into words what I was thinking.

Livvy shook her head, and started greedily on her omelette. "No he didn't have any designs on me, if that's what you're thinking."

"Charlie wasn't a tattoo artist then."

Livvy didn't catch the joke so I didn't bother explaining it.

"There wasn't much left to eat in the house."

"In the house?" I watched her eating.

"Yes, it was that farm we ran to for help, would you believe." She took a gulp of coffee.

I stared at her while she explained through mouthfuls of food how the police having taken the farmer into custody had left the farmhouse unattended and Charlie had merely broken in and made himself at home.

If there was food in the house which she thought there must be, Charlie had kept most of it for himself.

I swore. "So that's where he made the calls to me from, cunning bugger."

Livvy nodded a yes, stifling a yawn.

" I think you should take the day off work tomorrow, that's if you are due to work tomorrow?"

"No, I'm not expected in until next Monday, though I'd rather be at work than go through another police interrogation."

I smiled at her description of a police interview.

"I suppose I will have to face another one?" her look asked me to say no.

Instead I said, "Not if you are strong enough to avoid one at this stage as I mean to do."

She drew her brows together. "What do you mean?"

I said, "I mean to be out of here very early in the morning before the phone rings requesting the pleasure of my company, just on the off chance a certain policeman believes I might be involved."

"Out to where? West"

"To a certain building site in the Borders, for somehow I think that is where we will find our missing Mark Lauder."

Livvy's eyes opened wide. "You really think Mark is alive and could be there?"

"I believe so. Now are you fit enough to travel?"

"Fit enough to burst you mean," Livvy rose, "I suppose I better get my beauty sleep."

Looking at her slim figure I dare not say that she could keep me awake all night if that was the case. Naturally I did not dare as I still valued my front teeth.

Chapter 9

We left close on 6am before the Force had started its morning coffee. I thought it interesting to retrace the route I thought the abductors of Mark and Martin Quinn had taken on their way to the Borders should my theory prove correct.

I only had a vague idea where the body of the actor had been found from Thomson's brief reference that it was close to Whiteadder Reservoir in the Lammermuir hills.

It was not quite daylight by the time I reached what I thought was roughly the spot where Mark's car and Martin Quinn's body had been found. Braving the flurries of snow I got out the car and Livvy followed. She shivered and drew up the collar of her jacket.

"Is this the place?" Livvy looked dejectedly around her at the desolate eerie scene, all quite different in summer of course.

I shrugged, "could be." I took a few steps forward and looked around.

"Why here, West?"

"It wasn't planned Livvy. I think Wee Martin just fell into a coma from lack of insulin. I for one did not know he was a diabetic until I found the empty syringe in his bedroom the night he was abducted. He kept that well hidden for fear of someone knowing that the real Andrew Muir was not diabetic. Though like you and Mark we had never met the real Andrew Muir, and as our job was to keep everyone away from him there was little chance of this being discovered."

Livvy nodded her understanding. "Also you had to keep his grandchildren away for they would have instantly recognised Martin as a phoney."

"Yes that too. No one was allowed to see him from his Company, including your teasing of a certain little message boy."

Livvy laughed. "That was funny."

"Not to him. The poor kid's probably mentally scarred for life, especially you asking him if he would like a piece of your cherry…"

"Cake!" Livvy howled. "My cherry cake!"

We were still laughing when we got back into the car. The first time I remember us laughing together, at least for a while.

I followed the road through Cranshaws to Preston, turning on to the A 6112 and so on to Duns and eventually the new residential site outside of Wark. We stopped in that town to have a meal in a hotel before making our way to the site of Muir's new housing estate, of Birkshaven.

I drew up a little distance away from the cabin that obviously acted as the office.

"You remember your part? You and I are a couple looking for a three bedroom detached villa."

"Okay." Livvy shivered a little.

"Cold?"

"No, a little nervous. What if you're wrong and Mark's not here at all. Maybe even.." she stopped, leaving the rest of her thoughts unsaid.

"Well at least it won't be long until we find out."

We watched one man push a barrow up a plank and into one of the few partially completed houses, the remainder of perhaps forty or so which were scarcely beyond the foundation stage. No one else seemed to be about, the whole place eerily quiet for what should have been a hive of activity.

We got out the car and walked to the office. "Not much going on for a construction site," Livvy commented drily.

"Only so much you can do in weather like this," I said unconvincingly.

I knocked on the door and waited until it opened to reveal a young man standing there.

"Good afternoon," his smile clearly saying that he was glad to see someone…anyone to alleviate the boredom.

"Good afternoon to you too," I replied returning his smile."My wife and I are interested in your estate here as we are thinking of moving into the district."

My explanation must have satisfied him for he stood aside and ushered us into his small but brightly lit office.

"Very cold today, I'm surprised anyone is out at all."

Still smiling he slid down into a swivel chair behind his desk, his two bar electric fire close at hand, or should I say feet.

"Perhaps I should introduce myself, my names Harry."

"Mr and Mrs Kerr." I responded

"So you are considering coming to live in this area?" He waited for my reply and no doubt my reason, which I chose to ignore, experience having taught me that you were apt to trip up over too many fabrications, or should that be lies.

Livvy came to my rescue. "Have you any brochures that we may take a look at?" she gave the young salesman one of her most engaging 'cherry cake' smiles.

Scarcely able to tear his eyes away, the man searched the top of his desk for an appropriate sample. Finding one he handed it to her.

Livvy opened it sharing it with me.

For a minute or two we read the brochure with the photo of the completed show house on the front.

"There is one completely fitted at present as a show house. I can show you through it if you are interested. We have six detached villas in construction at the moment. Unfortunately all are already sold. There are however another six due to be completed by March and should you be interested, I have been instructed to offer any interested party the same design at today's price.

Livvy looked up from the brochure feigning interest. "And that price would be?"

"650K"

"I think we could manage the k" I said flippantly.

Harry's smile said he was not going to get a sale from this wise guy. However he was going to give it a damned good try on this dreary dismal day for he had nothing else to digest, except perhaps his afternoon's sandwich.

"We have nine three bedroom semi detached houses at a much lower price of 499K" He raised his eyebrows in a manner that all good sales persons do when meaning to say 'surely you can afford that' or, so as not to have insulted their potential client end with 'perhaps that's not what you had in mind? All are subject to 10% deposit of course."

"Of course," I said, further annoying the young man.

"You say these houses will be completed by March?" Livvy stared out the window at the deserted site. "Not at this rate I expect."

Harry looked uneasy. "It's the weather at present. As soon as it clears there will be more working on site. At present there's only a skeleton crew."

"Don't you feed them Harry," I laughed though feeling guilty at wasting the young man's time, after all he was only trying to make a living and here was I leading him on.

I quickly changed tact. "Does Davie Campbell come here often?"

Surprised by the question and my use of Campbell's first name, Harry drew back all the better to study me.

"You know Mr Campbell?"

"We worked for him while looking after Mr Muir," Livvy explained.

Although impressed, Harry was also embarrassed as what to say next regarding the publicity surrounding the death of Martin Quinn and all that it had entailed.

"No Mr Campbell has not been here for some time."

"You must be very clever to run all this on your own." Livvy gave the young man one of her enchanting smiles.

Harry coloured slightly at the compliment. "I share the time with Duncan. He's due back from lunch at about now."

I stood up. "We better let you have yours then. Sorry to have wasted you time pal, but I think these houses are well out of our league, unless you have an offer of, buy one get one free."

Harry pretended to appreciate my quip, though probably fuming inside and wishing all sorts of nasty things he would like to do to me.

Harry and Livvy rose together. "Have you a card you can give us, on the off chance that we may reconsider?"she asked.

"Of course." Harry reached into his jacket pocket and handed Livvy a small business card. "My name and business phone number are on it."

"Thank you Harry. We will surely ask for you if we do. You have been most kind." She offered him her hand which he took eagerly, his failure to make a sale already forgotten or put on hold until 'my wife' and I had departed.

Once back in the car, Livvy turned to me. "A right waste of time that was." She sounded annoyed.

"Oh I don't know. At least we know none of the bosses are around, and this place will be as dead as a graveyard at night."

"You don't expect to find Mark in one of those houses do you?"

I laughed, "Not unless it's the show house." Livvy tugged furiously at my sleeve. "Only kidding girl."

Agitatedly Livvy pointed at someone making for his car.

"What?" I followed her pointing finger.

"Look! He's wearing Mark's coat. The one I bought him for the winter."

Livvy's suspect had reached his car. "You sure about this Livvy? There must be other coats the same." I switched on the engine.

Excited now Livvy nodded eagerly. "Maybe so, but there are not many wearing Canada Goose.!" She stamped her feet. "He's getting away, West, follow him for God's sake."

"Don't get too carried away. Let's give him a wee start before we go after him."

I let the car almost reach the main road before I started after him. He was not heading in the direction of the main town but to the outer suburbs.

A few minutes later he turned into a very prosperous street, should the size of the houses be anything to go by. I halted and waited at the corner while he drove his car up the driveway of a large stone Georgian style house.

"Not short of a bob," Livvy said softly.

"Yes. Could be that coat's his very own." I said flippantly.

To hide her displeasure at my remark, she said angrily,

"Are we just going to sit here all day and do nothing?"

"Yip. Or at least until it's dark." I glanced at my watch, "which should be in about an hour's time. Put on the radio if you are bored."

"Goodie goodie, that should help the time fly past."

I fumbled in my jacket pocket. "Would you like a saft mint tae sook, hen?"

Livvy drew me a look, annoyed by my flippancy. "I hear your vocabulary is improving."

"Oh I've always been bi- lingual as learned in the West on how fur tae speak Inglish."

Livvy saw the joke and gave a short laugh.

Serious, I explained. "We'll wait until dark before we make our way up the drive, by then we might catch him at his tea, that's of course if it is his house and he's not just visiting. Or hopefully he's on his own."

"Any more optimistic deductions, esteemed, detective?" Livvy was getting close to boiling point.

"Give me until its dark to think of a few more." I sat back in my seat and closed my eyes.

"Men." I heard from the voice beside me.

An hour later much to Livvy's relief we left the car.

Keeping to the shadows on the edge of the driveway we made a silent approach to the house. At the corner I stopped. "Wait here Livvy where you can keep an eye on the front door. Keep in the bushes. Should anyone leave, come and tell me, I will be snooping round the back. Okay?"

I left her and stepped quietly along the side of the grey stone walled house. The windows that were lit were too high for me to see through, but once round the corner a window that looked very much like the kitchen was on a level for me to peer into, which I did very carefully, but saw no sign of life, although I thought I heard music somewhere in the background.

A little further, steps led up to the back door. Optimistically I tried the big iron handle, but without success, so much for optimism. Down the steps again and into a not very well kept garden I explored further. At little below ground level at what I guessed could be a cellar, one window was heavily barred and shuttered with only the slightest hint of light showing.

Could this be where my pal Mark was held? Or was I entirely wrong? Did the owner merely work on the building site?

I returned to where I had left Livvy.

"Did you find anything?"she asked eagerly.

"A cellar with shutters and a barred window."

She looked in the direction of the back garden. "You think Mark could be there?"

I breathed warm air into my cupped hands. "No way in knowing.

"So what do we do now, West? Come on you're the expert." Livvy's voice had an edge to it.

I threw my hands in the air. "I could knock on the front door and ask if Mark is coming out to play. Let me think Livvy."

"Not a good time to start."

"Not funny, girl."

"Okay. Wait here. There's no way into the house except by the front door."

"Are you thinking he might invite you in?"

"Yes, if my plan works."

I left Livvy waiting in the shadows, the outline of a plan in my mind. I would appear to be looking for someone in the neighbourhood and ask if he could help me.

I ran up the six or seven stone steps to his front door, rang the bell and waited.

It took a few minutes before a light was switched on and through the glass panelling of the front door the shape of a man appeared.

For a few seconds he stood there, then without warning the door flew open and before I knew what literally hit me I was bouncing down the stairs, rib cage on rib cage.

I must have blacked out for the next thing I remember was Livvy anxiously looking down into my upturned face, the pain in my head like the thumping music from a teenager's car radio.

"West! West! Are you all right?"

Stupid thing to say I thought, but in no position physically or mentally to give it the answer it deserved.

Livvy helped me while I shakily got to my feet. I was still not sure where I was or what had happened.

"He's got away West!" Angrily she pointed to where our suspects car had stood in the driveway.

I cursed, the obscenity hurting my brain. I should have blocked the driveway with my car while I explored. Now it was too late.

I leaned on her shoulder. "No worries. He won't get far after we tell the cops."

Livvy swung in the direction of the house. "His running away can only mean Mark must be in there."

Weakly I drew her back before she headed towards the house. "Hold on Livvy, what makes you think there was only one in there." Although I did not think so, it gave me time to gather my aching ribs and head together and stop this excited girl from rushing in where fools like me feared to tread.

Whoever he was that hit me had done so because he had recognised me, so much so that he had taken to his heels, or in this case his car without a backward glance, or taken the time to gather anything before making his rapid getaway. To leave everything behind must mean that he was into something very deep.

"West!" Livvy was urging me. Now there was no concern for my welfare, only anxiety for her beloved Mark. I swore under my breath at such loyalty, not to mention love.

I led the way into the house, silent except for the sound of music somewhere. A few hasty searches of the rooms confirmed that there was no one else except ourselves.

Livvy stared at me expecting me to have the answer to it all. "He's not here! Mark's not here! Bugger it!" She sat down heavily on a settee in the lounge.

"We haven't tried the cellar. You know, the one where I saw the barred windows."

Livvy flew to her feet. "That's right, he's got to be downstairs" She was out the door before my laboured breathing could stop her.

"Where's the bloody door?" I heard her cry from somewhere.

"Where are you?"

"Here!" she shouted and I followed the sound.

When I found her she was looking at a bolted door at the end of a passageway.

For once my impatient partner remained silent. She looked at me then; her hands trembling pulled back the bolt and opened the door.

All that greeted us was blackness.

"Hold on." I drew my hand down the door jamb and

found the light switch. "That's better." I took a step into what previously had been a black void, now lit it revealed a short passageway, another door at its end, again closed with a bolt.

"My turn." I drew back the bolt, trepidation having me shake at what I might find. The music had stopped, there was someone on the other side.

I was met with the sight of a large bare room, bare that is with the exception of one chair. a bucket in the corner, a transistor radio on a small table in the corner, and the startled dishevelled figure of Mark rising from where he had been sitting to meet me us both, between us a high wooden table jammed across the door where I stood.

"Mark!" I shouted, at the same time as he called out both our names.

"How did you find me?" He came as close as the table that blocked the entrance would allow.

"Never mind that for now. First, let's move this monstrosity out of the way." I put my hand under the lip. "It won't budge."

"I know. It's too damned heavy. And not the right height for me to climb up on and kick the bastard that brings me my meals, if you can call them that."

"Oh Mark! What have they done to you?" Close to tears her usual resilience all but gone, Livvy sobbed, her eyes never leaving the figure of the man she undoubtedly loved.

With three of us manhandling the huge mahogany table that had acted as a safety barrier when Mark had been given his meals eventually moved aside, the two lovers were instantly in each other's arms.

Mark was the first to release his hold and take a step back. "What's all this about, Livvy?" He looked old in comparison to the last time I had seen him and his voice was strained.

"First, let's get you upstairs." I said.

In the lounge Livvy rushed to the phone.

"Who are aiming to call, Livvy?" I asked as she stood there phone in hand.

"The police. Who else?"

I shook my head. "Not quite yet. Do you want to go through another 'interrogation'?"

Livvy dropped the phone into its cradle with a thud. "Bloody hell, no."

I took control. "See if you can find Mark a bite to eat. I'll find something for him to wear."

I looked at his far from tidy appearance, dirty to be precise. "Go wash up. I'll find you something to wear. No offence pal but you stink to high heaven."

"So would you pal if you never saw a wash basin for as long as I have."

It had not been the most diplomatic thing to say, after all I suspected he'd been through, but it had to be said. Although I was sorely tempted to have the local cops see and smell him, as he was at present.

"Sorry."

"Okay West. But tell me where the hell am I for god's sake and why?"

"You're in the Borders near Wark. As to why is a long story. Lets get something into you first. Now go and wash up."

. "You do look as if you are starving Mark, I'll search around." Livvy shooed him out of the room.

The house was large with at least seven rooms. It was in a desk drawer in what I thought must be the study that I came upon a phone bill bearing the name of James Shaw, who was more than likely to be the owner, unless the house was rented which it could be, remembering how quickly our Mr Shaw was in leaving it all behind him. However a few more papers confirmed him as the owner.

Upstairs I found a wardrobe full of some very classy suits, shoes and what I was most looking for, shirts.

Shirt in hand I entered the kitchen where Livvy was hard at work frying bacon and eggs, the smell inviting.

"That's better," Mark announced, coming in.

"My cooking or your wash?" Livvy could not hold back her joy at finding Mark again.

"Both." Mark sat down at the table. He turned to me. "I should be phoning Margaret to let her know I am well. I can't wait to hear Kirsty's voice again."

The stress and anxiety in his voice was unmistakable, only the policeman in him had prevented him from charging when first released to the phone and telling Margaret and Kirsty he was alright.

"Do that as soon as you've eaten."

Livvy put a full plate in front of him and Mark started eagerly. "There's not enough bacon for two," she apologised to me.

"Tea and a sandwich will do me for now. What about you? You haven't eaten since we had that meal in town."

"I'll have the same as you."

I sat down across the table from Mark. "Tell me what happened to you."

Mark chewed a piece of bread, and began.

"It was the night you phoned and said you'd be late. When I heard a car in the drive I naturally thought it was you, but instead opened the door to two masked men. Before I knew what was happening I was bundled into the boot of a car, which I knew was not my own as it was much too large. What they were after I don't know, but I hazard a guess that it was something to do with Mr Muir."

I nodded and watched him gulp down his tea.

"You're right there. But go on." My look told Livvy not to interrupt.

"I had no idea where we were going. I tried unsuccessfully to prise open the boot but had no success. However I did guess that we were on an empty country road. At length we stopped. After a while I heard the passenger door open and close and we continued on our way for what seemed ages and I was bursting for the toilet" For the first time I heard Mark laugh in a way I had always known him to.

"Blindfolded I was thrown into a room. When I took the blindfold off, it was to find myself in the cellar you found me in."

"You poor man." Livvy choked.

"We won't go into details now Mark, it will save you telling them all again to the cops. Only you should know that Martin Quinn was the man they also abducted."

"Martin Quinn?"

"Quinn was an old actor who was playing the part of our Mr Muir, who we were supposed to be guarding, the reasons for such still escapes me."

I threw Livvy a look that said, now for the hard part. "I don't know whether you knew this or not, but Martin Quinn was a diabetic?" Mark shook his head, and I went on, "Where you stopped was in the Lammermuirs near Whiteadder Reservoir. Martin Quinn died there from a diabetic coma."

"Christ!" Mark exploded. "I had an idea there was only the driver and myself in the car at first. So this man Quinn …"

"Was in your car, Mark." Livvy explained.

"And my car?"

"Thomson's holding it for safekeeping at present." Mark understood what I meant.

I rose suddenly. "Right, Mark go and do your phoning, while Livvy and I clear up here. We don't want the fuzz thinking we have not informed them straight away regarding our swift departing kidnapper Mr James Shaw.

It was after midnight before I drove into Mark's street, he and Livvy were still asleep in the back seat. Wrapped up together in Mark's expensive coat, they had finally exhausted themselves over the 'Muir affair.

At first we had gone over with the police what had happened at the house. They had taken statements while forensics searched the house for further evidence. Also I told them that should they need further information they should contact a certain DC Thomson at Fettes.

After Mark had refused to see their doctor, and understanding how anxious he was to see his daughter, the police eventually let us all go. He however would have to call at the Hawick police station to make a formal statement.

Margaret opened the door and tearfully fell into her brother's arms.

Softly we made our way into the lounge where a sleeping little girl lay on the settee covered by a tartan travelling rug.

Mark tip toed across the floor to stare down at the wee girl he had not seen for what to him must appeared to be years instead of weeks. Kirsty gave a slight cough and turned on her side. Mark smiled down at her. There must have been some sort of infinity between them for suddenly her eyes were open and she was shouting, "Daddy! Daddy!" Kirsty was in her father's arms, all sign of tiredness gone.

A little later after thanks from all, especially Mark at his release, I was on my way home.

Now I knew where my next step would be.

Chapter 10

The moment I stepped off the plane I felt it warmer than Edinburgh. Perhaps it was the lack of air quality, or just the location on the map. However, it was not sufficiently warm to be without a coat, which thankfully I was not.

After leaving Heathrow Airport, that thriving and busy anthill of people, not a few of whom were searching for lost luggage, only to discover once having found it that they themselves were now lost, I made my way to Piccadilly Circus via the underground.

Creada I found was located just off upper class Cleveland Place, all glass front and potted indoor flowers in a foyer large enough to hold a five a side football match...well almost.

The attractive young lady behind the reception desk already had her practised smile in place before I was half way across the tiled floor.

"Good afternoon sir. May I help you?" her smile lit up even more as she surveyed this handsome young Scot before her, or so I hoped.

"Good afternoon to you to," I hoped my smile matched hers, "I had a look at your website advertising your property abroad. Majorca mainly. Can you help me?" I smiled even broader.

"Of course sir." Her smile slackened long enough for her to consult something below the rim of her desk. "I believe Mister Cummings is free at the moment," she beamed up at me, "If you will give me a moment? Could I have your name sir?"

Only if you marry me I thought. "Barns. West Barns."

"Thank you sir."

She reached for her phone, and I turned to saunter through the surrounding opulence to pick up a brochure from a low glass topped table.

"Mister Barns, Mister Cummings can see you now." She had stood up to call across to me and pointed to the lift. "Third floor first door on your right."

"Thank you." I gave her the thumps up, which seemed not to have been in her manual on how to receive potential clients, the way her smile had faded, her bewildered expression saying uncouth Scot.

Following Miss' Smilie's' or should that be Miss Beamish's directions, I knocked upon the glass door which said S. Cummings Senior Manager, opening the door to a young man in his mid twenties. "Mister Cummings?"

Cummings rose. "Mister Barns, I believe." He held out his hand. I shook it and sat down in the proffered black leather chair. "Ms Fleming informed me that you may be interested in one of our Majorca properties?"

"Could be, Mister Cummings. It depends entirely on where they are."

"Quite." Our Mr Cummings unfolded a large coloured brochure depicting pictures of white walled red terracotta roof tiled villas. He pointed to the middle of the brochure. "This complex is already completed. Unfortunately they are all sold." He offered me a smile which was not in the same league as his receptionist. "However we do have others in the process of construction which are close to the little town of Petri and conveniently close to the beach."

"Not by rocket?" I joked.

Cummings looked at me as though I was mad, and I looked at him as if I wasn't.

"No, Mr West, only a few minutes' walk, I can assure

you."

I made a sound of apology. "So should I be interested, what next?"

Cummings face lit up at the promise of a sale. "When you have decided on which size property you prefer, and should your credentials prove satisfactory, we will ask for a 10% deposit."

I nodded that I understood. "When do you expect completion of these villas?" I took a look at his brochure in the same way I had in the Birkshaven estate back in Wark.

"Most probably March or April."

Same as Birkshaven I thought. "Do you have any literature on the Company?" was my next question.

For a moment my good Mr S Cummings looked taken aback.

"Should I decide to spend my hard earned savings on such a venture, it would be in the knowledge that your company is well established."I explained.

"Quite." Cummings drew out a drawer. "You will find our Company listed in Companies House, together with our assets. Also of Mr Anderson… a fellow Scot I believe, our Company Director."

I made a face that I was suitably impressed. I rose from my comfortable chair, and held out my hand across the desk to Cummings who stood up to shake it and said, "I hope we can do business together Mr West. I am sure you will be more than happy with the completed property. When you have, you can also decide on which site you prefer, as there are quite a few of similar size."

With that we departed with me promising to be in touch should I be interested, which I was, but not in the same way as my good Mr Cummings thought.

Upon leaving Creada Pty Ltd, I treated myself to a slap up meal at one of London's slap up prices. On reaching the coffee stage I sat back and phoned brother Fenton.

It took the big mutt some time before answering,"What the hell do you want, West? You know I'm on holiday."

"Sorry big man but it's important or I wouldn't bother you, or whoever you might be with."

I heard him laugh. "How did you know?"

"I am still your wee brother you know. Besides I'm still a detective and have been trained in deduction."

"Well don't try deducting this call from your bill. But seriously, what's so important?"

Briefly, I related roughly what had happened since Mark and Martin Quinn's abduction, together with my suspicions of David Campbell's involvement, ending with the theory that the answer might lie in the Majorca town, Petri and could he meet me at Palma airport.

For a moment there was silence at the other end, although I was sure I heard a few muffled not too polite words.

"Okay wee brother." The sentence ended with a sigh, "What time am I to be there?"

"I'll get back to you when I find out the times of the flights."

"Make it tomorrow, I've something important to do tonight."

"What's her name?" I chuckled.

More muttered none too polite words on the other end. "You're too young to know that, wee brother."

"Okay I'll phone you," I took a look at my watch, "say around five tonight. That won't interfere with your meeting I hope?"

"Okay, five tonight, but no later."

Next morning I met Fenton at Palma airport. He gave me a wave and waited.

"Sorry if I have intruded into your love life, brother."

"Yes you looked distressed," he said flippantly.

We started to walk to where he had left his rented car. "This Petri is not too far away. I think we have time for a bite. Have you eaten?" Fenton opened his car door.

"Breakfast this morning. A snack on the plane here."

"Okay. We'll grab something on our way to Petri."

Petri was not so many miles from Palma. On the way I attempted to inform Fenton of what I knew and suspected.

"So you believe this Campbell guy is behind it all." Fenton steered his rented car round a slow moving tractor.

"Yes. It all started with Muir's idea of employing a double at his home in order to distract rival companies from a project he was reputedly interested in starting in the Highlands. Mark, his friend Livvy or myself had never met the man so we were easily taken in. This gave Campbell the opportunity he was looking for unknown to Muir, who was in the USA. Campbell had some time ago started a company in London with the name of Creada and under the assumed name of Anderson planned to build a complex here in Petri. The trouble was, Campbell never intended to build the sixty or so houses he had advertised to do. I saw one of those brochures myself," I explained, "A client was required to put down a 10% deposit. However I believe Campbell got too greedy and has done the same with his boss's site at Birkshaven near Wark."

"So why was Mark Lauder and this old guy Quinn abducted?" Fenton drew up at a red light, and I praised the way he handled this left hand drive car.

"While Quinn was playing at being Muir somehow he came upon a document which he was not supposed to. I caught a brief glimpse of this document myself and saw that the name was Creada. I believe Quinn realised how important this was."

"And he tried to blackmail Campbell," Fenton finished my assumption for me.

"Yes. However, Campbell decided to have Mark and Quinn abducted and held out of the way until the plan was completed. For this he employed the services of one Johnny Webster who was also running a drug business at the time….which is another story," I apologised.

"Not the same Johnny Webster that was the cause of Mark Lauder leaving the Force?"

I nodded "The one and the same. You can imagine the fun your DC Thomson had with that one."

"I can," Fenton chuckled, "So what now?"

"I think we should wait until we reach Petri, then I might be in a position to shed more light on the whole affair."

"Okay you're the boss, but where do I come in?"

"You're my backup just in case anything goes wrong."

Fenton sped along the highway. "Thanks a bundle, I wouldn't have missed this part of my holiday for the world."

A half mile or so from the beach we found the residential complex site of Creada Pty Ltd. One house stood almost complete another three dozen or so were scarcely past the foundation stage, similar to the site at Birkshaven.

We found the Creada office or what stood for the office which was nothing more than a large wooden cabin like structure, standing inside a wire fence.

"No expensive spared I see." Fenton remarked sarcastically.

"Let's see what's inside." I stood back.

Fenton rolled his eyes heavenwards. "You want me, an officer of the law to break in?"

"Something like that."

"And if I get caught?"

"You can tell them you have just solved an enormous fraud case."

"Which you of course have not yet solved yourself, brother, eh?"

While we had been speaking, Fenton's little tool kit had been at work, all of a sudden there was a click and the squeaking gate swung slowly back.

"After you my accomplice in crime," Fenton stood aside to let me lead the way.

Fenton's procedure was much the same in gaining access to the cabin.

"Not much here," Fenton looked despairingly around him.

I pulled out a desk drawer, rummaged through a few papers then closed it again.

Fenton threw a coloured brochure across the desk to me. "This any good?"

I picked it up. There on the front cover was the picture of the one and only completed show house, the one we saw outside.

"Sure is," I looked through the window at the derelict complex, "The brochure that I picked up in London showed the same picture. Obviously they have convinced clients into believing that it is one of the completed villas here."

"What do we do now?" Fenton sat down in the one and only metal seat, and by his tone wished that he had not agreed to help me. I could not blame him, considering what I thought he may have left behind him in Palma.

"Let's go to the village, they're sure to know something, for I bet Campbell had a few men from there working for him."

Once at the village we were put in contact with the Alcade or mayor. He was a small bald headed man in his fifties, whose greeting was anything but civil when we mentioned our interest in the Creada project.

"This man Campbell, he say that he has OK to build a holiday..how you say.."

"Complex?" Fenton assisted him.

"Very complex, senor," the mayor said in all seriousness.

I held in a chuckle. "Then this man Campbell say he would have to stop our men working there until more people buy casas . He cause much trouble here. Many of the men had given up good jobs to work for him."

I looked across at Fenton. "I bet it did."

"When did you last see this villano?"

"Two days ago senor."

Fenton raised his eyebrows and I let out a low whistle. "It figures he will want to get out of the country before his clients become suspicious."

"And while his unsuspecting boss is still in USA," I added hopefully, "Do you have any idea where he might be now?"

"Come senors, I have where he lives when he is here."

We followed the little man and his bad English to his house, and gratefully sipped a wine while he rummaged for the address.

Fenton smiled across at me."This is better." He took another sip of his wine. "You could make your trip last till the end of the week and accompany me back home. A few days of this weather will help buck you up."

I looked out at the sunshine, and the smell of the sea. "Tempting but I have a fraudster to find, not to mention what he has done to Mark Lauder."

Our host returned clutching two objects. "This is where he stays when he is here, senor."

I looked at the piece of paper he had handed me. "Porto Pollensa!"

"Yes, that man say he does not wish people to annoy him when he is here, so he stays far away up north in this island." Here he handed me his second item, a photograph. "This is me and Campbell. He use this for the local paper. Tell how our village will be rich when casas are built and many people come to spend money." The little man said something in Spanish which took no guessing as to be nothing other than a few naughty words.

"Well, what do you make of that, little brother?" Fenton sat down behind the wheel of his rented car.

"Campbell can't be alone in all this, Fenton."

"No," Fenton agreed, "There has to be someone who has ready access to the Muir money to finance Creada, and also has the opportunity of ciphering it to destinations unknown. Most likely countries where it would be more difficult to have the money returned to the UK. Have you anyone in mind that fits the bill?"

I stared unseeing out of the car window. "Sure have. A certain Mr Blair, accountant. It all fits. It could also be him who organised Mark and Quinn's abduction, especially if he had a hand in the drug business."

"You haven't told me about that, West."

"Okay, I will fill you in as best I can on the way to sunny Puerto Pollensa.

The address the little mayor had given me was on the Wandelen Boulevard, a little beyond the last pavement café, on the busy front of Puerto Pollensa.

"You don't get that back home." Fenton referred to the tables on the pavement.

"Oh yes you do," I countered, "but they're called evictions," I laughed.

Eventually we found the address, it was an apartment, which when looking through the iron gate appeared not to have been lived in for quite some time.

Fenton tried the gate and to our surprise it proved to be unlocked, and to our added surprise also the front door.

Fenton led the way, swiping away a few buzzing flies on his way to the front room.

There, a man with his back to us, sat in a high backed leather chair. Cautiously we approached him from either side.

Fenton was the first to speak. "He's dead, West. Shot through the head. Do you know him?"

I nodded, for I was looking down into the sightless eyes of David Campbell. I choked back my surprise. "That's Campbell, Mr Muir's managing director. How long would you say he's been dead?"

Fenton was already searching Campbell's pockets. "I'd say in this heat only about a couple of hours or so, Rigor Mortis has not yet set in." He stood back holding a passport and airline ticket. "So someone knew he was here and didn't want to share the ill gotten goods so to speak."

"Could only be Blair," I suggested.

"Or Muir himself."

I shook my head, "Somehow I think my money's on Blair."

"One way to find out, brother," Fenton crossed to the

window and gazed out at those lucky enough to be lying on the beach enjoying the sun. The happy chattering of those passing from having lunch under the canopy of their favourite restaurant, and although it was November and not at its hottest, it was still far warmer than the London I had left those short hours before.

I took out my mobile and fortunately the reception was not too bad.

"Good day, Muir Construction. How may I help you?" a polite female voice greeted me.

"I was hoping that it might be possible to speak to Mr Blair your accountant if it is not too inconvenient."

At the window Fenton rolled his eyes to the ceiling at my unusual politeness, before flicking open the airline ticket holder. I heard the voice at the other end say, "I am sorry sir, but Mr Blair is on vacation, and won't be back for another three weeks. Can someone else be of assistance?"

"No," I said more bluntly that intended, then in way of apology. "Thank you. You have been most helpful."

"Most convenient, wouldn't you say?" Fenton commented,

I sat down in a chair by the veranda, and said what I was still in the process of thinking. "Blair was careful to keep his hands clean by not being physically involved in the abduction of Mark and Martin Quinn, or to be in the location when Livvy and I were caught the night of finding the drugs, therefore I would say he now has to be desperate to have killed his partner."

"Or they just fell out," Fenton suggested, "It's not unknown. One seizes the chance to have it all, which has the added attraction of not having to live with the knowledge that your partner should he be caught may give you away for a lighter sentence."

I opened the airline folder made out in the name of David Campbell, "This is for a flight from Palma to Paris at 7 o'clock tonight." I said in surprise.

"You think Blair might also be on that flight?"

"Could be Fenton." I glanced at my watch. "If we were to leave now, we'd be at the terminal in plenty of time."

Fenton came away from the window. "Okay."

"What about here? Shouldn't we inform the local law?"

"If we do, you won't be in Palma for the kill, and your Mr Blair will leave free as a bird…not as you hoped, a jailbird."

I didn't laugh at my brother's joke, not that I was apt to do anyway. Instead I asked, "So what do you suggest?"

"First, let's get to the airport; from there inform the local constabulary where to find Campbell. Also briefly explain why we left the scene of a crime in an attempt to apprehend Blair, who only you know by sight."

I agreed and we set off, with me thinking how pleased Livvy would be not to be involved in another police 'interrogation'.

It was late afternoon when we reached the airport. I bought a couple of sandwiches while Fenton parked his rented car, my small overnight bag still in the boot.

By six thirty there was no sign of our Mr Blair around the appropriate departure gate. I saw a few police hovering around but did not as yet wish to make their acquaintance.

Fenton returned from looking at some other departing flights.

"Any sign?" I asked.

He shook his head. "Only cops could look at some of the flight lists. Although they would only have your description of Blair, that's if there are any here on the job.

Then again he might be already away under an assumed name, or perhaps has not planned to leave until tomorrow."

"Although assuming that it was he who killed Campbell, he'd want to leave Majorca as soon as possible. That's also assuming he had planned to kill his partner in the first place, which I'd say he had, as he shot Campbell through the head."

"Premeditated," I murmured.

We hung around the departure lounge until close on midnight, until the final flights had left. By that time we had made our acquaintance known to the police.

Disappointed that I should have failed to catch the man responsible for it all, Fenton his holiday at an end, he and I left the Majorca's sunshine for home three days later.

Blair had escaped.

Epilogue

We had chosen a quiet café off Chambers street to meet.

Giving the TV screen above the counter a brief glance Fenton lifted his coffee cup.

"What's DI Thomson saying to it all?" I asked, ready to be amused by my brother's answer.

"He thought he'd have a dig at me for letting Blair escape until I told him Majorca was hardly my patch and that I was merely there as a citizen on holiday."

I chuckled and studied my coffee cup. "What was his answer to that one?"

Fenton took a sip of coffee, "As expected he attempted to turn the situation around by blaming you and 'that woman' for interfering in his case."

"Interfering," I retorted, "We practically solved the case for him, despite him holding us back with those damned interrogations, as Livvy would say." Then seeing the humour of Thomson trying to nail down Livvy and me for the various interviews, I let out a laugh.

"He was right though," Fenton conceded. "You still have to answer a few charges."

Changing the subject my brother took another not too interested glance at the screen. "Pity though that he got clean away."

I knew that he meant Blair. Not that it was in any way my brother's fault but it rankled the policeman within him. No less myself.

"Muir despite his losses has seen Mark all right. Gave him quite a large sum for his ordeal. Livvy too, which I thought was good of him."

"And you, West?"

I shrugged. I hadn't wanted to say, but the way this certain police brother of mine was staring at me I knew that I was just as well to let him know now, rather than have him drag it out of me later, probably under the most embarrassing situations such as when dining a new lady friend in one of Edinburgh's best restaurants and he arrived to have me arrested, which I might add he had done on one previous occasion. "I gave Mark most of my fee. I can well afford it you know."

Fenton drew me a dry look. "That was nice of you, but that money your millionaire friend gave you for saving his sons' is not likely to last forever, adding tongue in cheek, "especially if you keep failing to catch the villain."

My answer though jovial was unprintable.

"What's your pal up to now? I bet it was a sight for sore eyes when he met his wee girl again." Fenton said cheerfully.

"It was, though she was fast asleep when we all arrived."

I don't know who it was that first noticed the café having gone suddenly quiet and everyone staring up at the TV screen.

"What the hell...." Fenton gasped as we both looked and listened to the news reporter. In the background, the pictures of a ferry lying almost totally submerged a few hundred yards from the shore of a South American town and he was explaining how it had happened late last night, and that over one hundred were feared drowned. Followed by photographs and the news reporter saying, "It has now been confirmed that there were four UK nationals drowned. They were Mr Ronald Adams and his wife and four year old daughter from Salisbury."

In the café some female voice said, "Poor souls."

"The other victim is believed to be businessman Ian Anderson from Edinburgh Scotland"

I gasped so loud that a few turned to stare."That's Blair! Fenton that's Blair!"

Fenton turned to stare at me. "You sure?"

"Of course. I met him at his office. I would know him anywhere." I was shaking, a myriad of thoughts flashing through my mind as I pointed at the screen.

"Poetic justice, would you not say brother? Gets away with a fortune then this."

Fenton nodded calmly at the screen, "All that money hidden somewhere in a foreign bank."

He stood up with a glance at his watch, "Well brother of mine, some of us have to work."

We had reached the door when I said. "So there's an end to it after all. At least I don't feel such a failure over it all now."

Fenton took a step away and turned to face me, "That's if it is Blair, and he was not a good swimmer." He beamed mischievously at me.

"Why don't you try that one on Thomson, Fenton. After all it was his case."

With this I bade my mischievous brother a fond farewell

The End.

Note to readers :

Most places are fictional as is the Spanish village of Petri and the building Company of Creada. All incidents although also fictional take place before the formation of Police Scotland and the introduction of the use of mobile phones in vehicles. Text messages were not always available at this period of time.

Printed in Great Britain
by Amazon